Potpourri

A Short Story Collection

By

Irene Ebel Ertell

To

Mother and Dad

Preface

Writing short stories began when I decided to preserve the story of our German family on my dad's side. Because I wanted to write a story my children would enjoy and appreciate, not just genealogical facts, I decided to take a class at the local community college to hone my writing skills. I had very little information on my forebears, so I started writing about what might have been for class assignments. I didn't use them in my published family story, but they whetted my appetite for writing short stories about people and happenings.

Before long I joined five other women writers. We met every other Thursday at someone's home to read and critique our work. After I published the family story, my interest in short stories continued. When I moved to a retirement center, I joined a Saturday morning writing group. Even without critiquing, it was a good place to get reaction and appreciation. I also had the opportunity to read my work to larger groups.

Though I composed on a computer, I made hard copies of everything. Generational mistrust of the cyberworld. When my file drawer began to complain at another addition, I decided to publish. That is what you hold in your hands. I ask you to remember that some of these stories were written twenty plus years ago. At any rate, I hope they take you to that other time, as they did me.

Stories

Around the Corner   1

A Different Christmas Gift   6

For the Love of Frannie   9

Taking Care of Mama   13

Jamal and Scheherazade   17

A Shove Out of the Nest   24

Mary's Ring   27

All's Fair in Love and Cooking   31

What's in a Word   34

Beyond Reach   36

Callie   38

Checking Out   42

The Escape   45

Joel   48

Guardian Spirit   52

The Exchange   59

Brother Ralph   62

Twenty-Fifth High School Reunion 69

Only a Little Bit 73

A Fine Cigar 76

Whither Thou Goest 79

Halloween Ball 82

Flash the Northern Flicker 86

The Piano 90

Four Friends 95

House for Sale 99

The Black Hole 103

Margot's Visitor 106

Mousey Brown 111

Snook and Maddie 115

Uncle Jasper 121

Memories 125

Prairie Life 128

River of Escape 138

Suzanne's Remote Revenge 143

When Things Go Bump in the Night   149

Scattered Flowers   151

The Visit   156

Watching, Waiting   161

When the Roll is Called Up Yonder   165

The Cat Caper   168

The Red Hat   172

Who Was That Man?   175

U-Turn   177

Yield Not to Temptation   183

Two Hearts   188

Around the Corner

They came from opposite directions and reached the café entrance at the same moment. A slender young man reached to open the door for a well-dressed young woman. She brushed past him without a glance or word of thanks. Irritation flushed the man's pallid cheeks, and he whispered to himself, "Bitch."

Noisy evening diners occupied all the booths and tables. Two places were left at the far end of the counter. He watched the auburn-haired woman stride, high heels clicking, hips swaying. She sat down. The man slowly walked to the remaining stool. As many times as he'd eaten here, he'd never seen her before.

They studied the menu chalked on a blackboard above the pass-through to the kitchen. The man brushed a strand of lank, brown hair from his forehead and pushed wire-rimmed glasses back on the bridge of his hawk-like nose.

When the woman turned toward him, he turned as well, thinking she meant to speak. Peering around the room, she looked straight through him.

"What'll it be?" demanded a frowsy, middle-aged waitress. She spoke to the man, but the woman answered. He had intended deferring to her as a courtesy when she cut him off.

"Chef's salad," she said.

"And you?" The waitress smirked.

"I'll have—" He noticed her hand poised below the woman's order. "We are not together." He emphasized "not together" and ordered the meatloaf special and coffee. The waitress gave him her "what a loser" look as she moved into the kitchen.

Again, the woman looked toward the man and inadvertently he turned. She looked past him to the front door that had opened. The next time the door opened, he managed to look straight ahead. He realized she must be waiting for someone.

"Damn," she muttered, glancing at a jeweled wristwatch.

The waitress brought their coffee. The woman picked up the sugar shaker and poured a good amount into her cup. When she shoved the shaker toward the young man, it began to tip. He reached to keep it upright and their hands touched. His body tingled.

"Sorry," she said in a low, whispery voice. He would have liked some sugar in his coffee but feared his hand would tremble.

As they waited for their food, the young man tried to look at the woman without turning his head. Just as he reached the limits of his peripheral vision, he was startled to see her watching him. She was smiling. He quickly ducked his head and focused on his cup of coffee. He knew she was still looking at him, but before he could think of something to say, the waitress brought their orders.

"Anything else?" She dared them.

"More coffee," the woman demanded, though her cup was half full.

2

The waitress filled the cup and turned to leave.

"You forgot the gentleman's," the woman snapped.

The waitress splashed coffee into his cup.

"Just a minute," the woman called, pointing a long red fingernail at a small spill on the counter. The waitress wiped it with the corner of her apron.

"High-class joint." The woman chuckled.

"The meatloaf is good," was all he could think to say. He felt the hot blush creeping up his neck.

The woman went at her salad with knife and fork. Her elbow brushed his jacket sleeve repeatedly, producing a remarkable sensation throughout his inner man. Meatloaf was one of his favorites, but he barely tasted it. The woman crossed her legs, setting off a rustle of hosiery against hosiery, surprising his deepest senses. He became aware of her perfume and inhaled deeply to prolong the pleasure. Daring to turn his head slightly, he saw how the neckline of her dress revealed a deep cleavage, round and creamy. Perspiration formed across his forehead.

Suddenly the woman grabbed his arm as she reached for the napkin that was slipping off her lap. When she began to slide from the stool, he stood to block her fall and encircled her with his arms. The softness of her body insinuated itself onto his chest where she lingered for a moment. Reluctantly, he helped her back onto the stool.

"Oh, thank you ever so much." She smiled and fluttered long eyelashes. He was tongue-tied. Now that he could look straight at her, he saw large green eyes, full red lips, and a patrician nose all set in a face of flawless skin. He didn't see the heavy makeup. Struggling to say something witty or urbane, he was relieved when the waitress slapped their checks down before the two plates.

"Anything else?" Without waiting for an answer, she moved along to another customer.

The woman rummaged in her handbag for a minute or so. "I think I must have left my wallet in another purse."

"Oh, uh, let me, uh, get your, uh, check." He was blushing. "Please?

"How sweet." She smiled at him.

She searched again, retrieving a pen and small white card on which she wrote something. As she got down from the stool, she placed the card in his lap, pressing it firmly below his belt buckle. The movement was practiced and unnoticeable to anyone else. All his senses came alive, and he had to grab the counter. She hurried to the front of the diner, high heels clicking.

Carefully he reached for the card. Printed in fine raised script he read: Darlene Tolman, No. 3 Lotus Lane. Scrawled below was: Around the corner. Give me ten minutes. The young man sat there, his heart pounding.

"Waitress," he called. "I'll have more coffee."

He kept checking his watch as he sipped. Finally, he got up and paid the two checks at the cashier's podium.

Night had fallen. City lights blazed and a cool breeze moved stray bits of paper and leaves along the sidewalk. Coming up the street was the bus he rode home every evening. The young man stood still for a moment, felt the small card in his pocket and then walked to the bus stop.

A Different Christmas Gift

Rapping on her apartment door awakened Val. Her clock gleamed 3:15. "I wonder if it's that new woman next door," she said. This would be the third time since she moved in last week.

The rapping continued, but not loud enough to disturb others who were sound asleep with their hearing aids on the night table. Val, a light sleeper, had become the prime target.

"Call us and we'll take care of it," said the night person on the downstairs desk. Yes, they came if she called, but they didn't do anything to keep Muriel Spooner in her room at night. So again, there she stood, smiling, naked as a jaybird except for high-heeled, silver sling-backs.

"How about a little nightcap?" She held a bottle of shampoo and two mugs.

Val took Muriel's hand and pulled her into the apartment, carefully settling her in a chair. She picked up the phone.

"Lynn? Muriel Spooner awakened me. No clothes."

"I'm so sorry, Mrs. Carstairs. We'll be right up."

Muriel opened the shampoo and poured the mugs full, insisting they do a chug-a-lug. Val put the bottle and mugs in the refrigerator.

"They will taste better after a good chill," she said.

Muriel giggled and crossed her bare legs.

Minutes later, the caregiver arrived, assuring Muriel they would have a nightcap as soon as she returned to her apartment. No one thought to bring a wrap, so Val grabbed one of her robes and the caregiver persuaded Muriel to wear it. That took several minutes because Muriel resisted strenuously.

The first night Muriel appeared, Val had no idea who she was. Later, Val discovered that Muriel's children had deposited their mother at the retirement center, assuring the staff she was capable of functioning as an independent resident. Extra care would have cost more.

During the day, Muriel stayed in her apartment. At meal times, she chose a two-person table and had little to say if anyone joined her. Val tried many times. Some nights, however, it was a different story.

When Christmas season approached, the staff and residents decorated the common areas and hallways. Fresh trees and garlands perfumed the air. Christmas carols and popular songs floated throughout the facility. Val and her neighbors noticed that Muriel's door remained bare, so they made a wreath. One day when Muriel was at lunch, Val and a friend hung it on her door.

Three days before Christmas, the center always held a celebration because most residents would still be there. Many had family in the area with whom they spent the holiday. Val volunteered to invite Muriel to go to the Christmas party. She accepted.

Muriel seemed at ease sitting at the table with Val and three others, though she didn't have much to say. After a sumptuous meal and dessert, a group of young people from the community came in and began to sing carols. Val was surprised when Muriel rose and walked toward the children. It was between songs, and she said something to them. Two singers in the front row moved over and Muriel stepped in beside them, turning to the audience with a big smile on her face. There was silence for a moment. The children began to sing Ave Maria. After a few bars, Muriel joined in. She sang softly, obviously not wanting to overpower the children. Her angelic soprano seemed to bring out the best in the children's voices. Muriel sang with the children until they finished. The applause was thunderous.

Christmas morning, rapping awakened Val at 3:15.

"Hi, Muriel," she said. "Come on in."

A carafe of wine and two stemmed glasses sat on the coffee table. A pink chenille robe lay draped over the back of a chair.

For the Love of Frannie

Frannie remembered the days when Jay, Virgie and Bebe sat on her, pulled her ears, used her tail for a pull toy and hugged her until her ribs ached. Frannie loved her children and never let them out of her sight when they played outdoors.

The Border Collie was so scrawny and scraggly, the shelter had decided to forego the adoption fee. Mom told her friends, "Frannie turned out to be the best babysitter we ever had."

After the children got older, the family rarely spoke to Frannie. When they did, it was, "get over here, no, Frannie, dumb dog." Except Bebe. "Good girl, Frannie. I love you, sweet doggie." Bebe still took time to scratch behind Frannie's ears, but she was seldom home. At different times, the children had begun going to a place called school. The small dog resigned herself to being alone and sometimes reminisced.

Frannie recalled the day her children and some of their friends were playing in the front yard. The older children were running in circles, laughing and yelling when Frannie saw Bebe toddling toward the street. Frannie heard a car and ran to grab the back of Bebe's playsuit with her teeth. The toddler whimpered as Frannie pulled her into the yard near the house.

More cars sped by. Frannie sensed danger and began to bark at the older children who continued to whoop and holler. Soon Mom came to the door and yelled.

"You kids get in the backyard this minute. If I've told you once, I've told you a million times to never play in the front yard. There are too many cars going too fast. Bring the baby." She watched to make sure they did as they were told.

After that, when the children strayed from the backyard, Frannie barked until Mom came and yelled. Frannie didn't like to hear Mom yell at the children, but she knew they would be safe.

In the winter, Frannie had been allowed to sleep at night in the laundry room because there was no heat in the garage. Early one morning, she awoke and smelled something strange. It was hard to breathe and her eyes burned. Frannie began to gasp but barked as loud as she could.

Dad came running and found the family room full of smoke. He and Mom poured lots of water on Dad's lounger. Jay, now tall and husky, helped them drag the smoldering chair into the backyard. The falling snow smothered the lingering smoke. They didn't call the Fire Department. "Our insurance would go sky high," said Dad. Frannie cringed when Mom yelled at Dad about his careless smoking. He called her a nervous Nellie.

Frannie's warning was forgotten by everyone except Bebe. She took Frannie out into the fresh air, scratched behind her ears and hugged her. Frannie licked Bebe's chin.

"Oh, Frannie, you are the smartest dog in the whole world," she said over and over. Bebe hid Frannie under her bed covers the rest of the night. After that, the laundry room became Frannie's bedroom. Bebe saved up to buy her a doggie bed.

As the years passed, Frannie became slower and tried not to move the parts that hurt. Some days it was easier not to eat, just lap a little water. Sleep was best.

"Mom, I'm really worried about Frannie. I think she's in a lot of pain. She can hardly go outside to do her business." Bebe had this conversation with her mother before.

"She's old, Bebe. She's thirteen or fourteen now." Mom said again.

"Maybe I should take her to Dr. Sam?"

"You'll have to ask Dad. Veterinarians aren't cheap."

"But Mom. She's such a good dog. Like a member of the family."

"Well, I wouldn't say that." Mom smiled. "Ask your Dad."

"Your Mom's right. Vets are expensive. He'll just tell us Frannie is old and her time is coming. That's the way things are." Dad lit a cigarette, pushed back in his lounge chair and turned on the TV.

The next day Frannie shivered when Bebe and Virgie wrapped her in her blanket and placed her on the back seat of the car. Virgie got behind the wheel. Bebe sat in back with Frannie, soothing her when she shivered.

"Thanks for helping, Virgie. Mom and Dad don't seem to care."

"There isn't money for extras with Jay and me in college at the same time. You'll be going year after next so there'll still be two of us in school. We're lucky they help as much as they do."

"I know." Bebe sighed. "Dr. Sam thinks Frannie has dysplasia, but he needs to examine her. If that's all she has, he says we can probably keep her comfortable until her time comes. Otherwise ... oh, Virgie." Tears rolled down Bebe's cheeks. Frannie snuggled her head into Bebe's lap.

"I know it's tough, little sister, but be glad that Dr. Sam is giving you a part-time job to pay for all this."

"I know," Bebe said. Frannie raised up and licked Bebe's chin.

Taking Care of Mama

"Hello, Patsy. What's on your mind?

"I hate it when you do that, Maybelle. I know you've got caller ID."

"Oh, for crying out loud. Just tell me what you want this time."

"Mama's started smoking again."

"Smoking? Cigarettes?"

"Of course, cigarettes."

"How'd you find out?"

"Joe Ray and I drove over to the home today? We were going to take her to lunch? I had called her last night and of course, I had to apologize all over the place. She was really wound up. 'I began to think you'd forgotten your poor old mother.' I reminded her that we'd visited her two weeks ago, but she just couldn't resist picking on me, like always."

"Patsy! How do you know she's smoking?"

"You always have to interrupt, don't you? Miss High and Mighty. When's the last time you went out to see her?"

"If you don't tell me about Mama's smoking, I'm gonna hang up."

"Well, when we got there, her door was locked. I had to knock and knock. She finally opened up, still in her nightgown. 'Well, look who's here,' she said, like she was surprised to see me? When I stepped into that room, the smell nearly knocked me over."

"What do you mean?"

"Cigarette smoke, I told you. The place reeked. Mama made out like she didn't smell a thing. Said it was 'just aroma de old folks home.'"

"Good grief, Patsy. You know Mama's got a sense of humor sometimes."

"Sense of humor, my foot. She glared at me and plopped herself down on the couch."

"Did she go to lunch with you?"

"Well, that was something else. Said she didn't remember my call. Then she couldn't decide what to wear. Took her good old time putting on all that makeup too. I knew Joe Ray was ready to explode. Waiting isn't his strong suit and ..."

"Patsy! I've got the picture. What else?"

"When we finally got downstairs, Joe Ray was walking up and down in the lobby. His face was all blotchy like he gets when he's holding it in."

"What did he say?"

"Nothing, thank goodness, but he tore out of that driveway like we were going to a fire."

"He drives that way all the time, Patsy."

"Well, Mama didn't help none. You know how she always insists on sitting up front? Says the back seat makes her queasy? Well, today she refused to get in the front. Said the front seat made her nervous because she could see Joe Ray's driving."

"She hit the nail on the head that time."

"Maybelle Graham, you're getting to be as bad as Mama. If you and Clovis paid her more attention, she wouldn't be so hard to get along with. Or at least it would spread it out."

"It was your and Joe Ray's idea to stick her way out there in the first place, so you could have the house all to yourselves. Besides, driving on the freeway makes me nervous. Clovis is gone most of the time trying to keep his towing business going. When he does come home, it's a six-pack of Bud and TV."

"Same old song, Maybelle, but the question remains. What do we do about Mama's smoking?"

"Did ya'll talk to her about it?"

"Lord knows I tried, but she just looked at me like I was from another planet and asked me to pass the cornbread."

"Patsy, don't you remember when we were little and she and Daddy stopped smoking? That's been forty plus years ago. Why would she start again? She couldn't stand cigarettes after she got over the habit. Always made a big deal about her battle with nicotine."

"True, of course. I told you how she was today, maybe she's going into Alzheimer's. Oh, Maybelle, what'll we do?"

"Control yourself, Patsy. Don't borrow trouble. There's an explanation. I'll call and see what she has to say."

Meanwhile, at Mama's apartment.

"Phew, Lila. It smells like a barroom in here."

"Sorry, Fanny. I been spraying, but it still stinks, don't it?"

"I should say. How'd you get it like this?"

"I asked Joe Sparks to come in this morning and smoke a few before Patsy got here. He kind of overdid it."

"Did ya'll go to lunch like you told me?"

"Yes, and Patsy wondered what in tarnation was going on, but I wouldn't tell her. Guess Maybelle'll be calling any minute."

"Why on earth did you do something like this?"

"Fanny, a Mama does what a Mama's got to do."

Jamal and Scheherazade

"I am sorry to tell you this, but it isn't possible to do the surgery for Scheherazade's left eye."

Jamal gasped in disbelief; his olive skin flushed deeply.

"But you said the eye had healed, and she would—with surgery—have good sight." His accent deepened. "She is blind already in the right eye!" That eye lost its vision to unknown trauma inflicted before Jamal found the little dog abandoned in a park five years ago.

He clamped his jaws shut to keep from screaming; fists clenched at his sides. Remembering. Three weeks before, the doctor suggested costly surgery which he couldn't afford. Now, when Jamal had found a way to get the money, this doctor said he wouldn't save Zadie's sight! Curse him!

As reason returned, the young man's shoulders slumped. He bowed his head for a moment before fixing his eyes on the doctor. Dr. Norris did not look away, recognizing the depth of Jamal's distress.

"We have received the presurgical test results," the doctor said gently, clearly. "They show that Scheherazade has diabetes. We can treat her with insulin and a special diet so that she can live comfortably for a good while in much the same way people live with diabetes. On the other hand, the disease could shorten her life considerably. In no case will I do the surgery. You may wish to consult with others to be sure."

"She will be blind?"

"Yes."

"Blind and sick," Jamal whispered as he turned and left.

"So, Zadie, what do we do?"

With the white, fuzzy-faced dog tucked beneath an arm, he slowly walked across the parking lot toward a red Ferrari; its soft, gray top, recently vandalized and repaired with duct tape.

Jamal was five feet nine or so; compact but not heavy. His black hair was groomed in a soft pompadour with medium sideburns, and a neat almost-to-the-collar trim. His heavy eyebrows shadowed deep-set eyes filled with tears. He wore a well-tailored business suit.

Brushing away the tears, he started the engine and slowly exited the Animal Eye Clinic parking lot as the street lights began to come on.

"First it is money. Now it is this diabetes. What else can happen to us now that all else is gone?" He spoke an Arabic dialect, gently scratching Zadie's arched back.

Jamal remembered another time when he felt despair. Contrary to his promise to his father, he remained in the United States after finishing his studies at the Massachusetts Institute of Technology. His father cut him off from all family contact, but youthful optimism persuaded him that one day his father would relent. Then the message came saying that his father died unexpectedly, and Jamal would not be welcome at the funeral. He decided to become an

American citizen and seek success. He would show them! Nevertheless, he continued to feel the loss keenly six years later and sometimes questioned the decision to break his filial promise.

The sky was dark and the breeze was cold when they arrived at the apartment complex. It took numerous twists and turns to find their lodgings. Brown leaves swirled around the open carport where he parked.

Jamal made certain the leash was secure before Scheherazade jumped to the pavement and led him to a designated grassy area where she relieved herself. They climbed the stairs to a second-floor apartment. After unlatching two heavy locks, he turned on a switch that lighted the narrow hallway and living room at the end of the hall. He reached into the kitchen and turned on that light too. Scheherazade trotted over to her water bowl and lapped thirstily.

Jamal changed into comfortable clothes and went to the kitchen. He opened the narrow pantry that held canned goods, drinks and Scheherazade's food. When the little dog heard the dry pellets echo in the plastic bowl, she came trotting.

"You are hungry, Zadie? Good girl. Bon appétit."

Reaching into the pantry he brought out a half-full bottle of vodka. He acquired this habit in America after giving up his tenuous belief in the Muslim religion. He didn't drink every night like so many of his expatriate countrymen, but there were times when the soothing effects of hard liquor were welcome. This was a time.

Jamal sat in his lounge chair. Just as he took a large swallow, the telephone across the room rang. It made him jump. He decided not to answer. He didn't want to talk to anyone. If it was important, let them leave a message. There would be no job offers this time of night.

"Al, this is Jeanine. I haven't seen you in some time and wondered if we might get together. I know you were put out with me after our last date, but you never gave me a chance to explain. I've missed you. I really have. Please call me, 645-8320. I hope to hear from you soon. Bye."

"Bitch!" he snarled. Hell would freeze over before she heard from him. How did she get his new number? If she realized what part of town he lived in now, she would have never called. She wanted something and didn't know that he no longer had the means to keep her happy. Expensive things made Jeanine happy and he kept her very happy until she met someone she thought could outdo Jamal.

Scheherazade finished her dinner and came into the living room where she sat on the floor in front of Jamal. He patted the seat next to him. She leaped up and positioned herself comfortably with her chin on his thigh. He scratched behind her ears.

Jeanine's call prompted recollections Jamal preferred to forget. After getting his degree, Jamal was hired by a Saudi Arabian based petroleum company in the United States. He worked hard and rose to a vice-presidency. Life was good and he lived it to the hilt until the day his company was found guilty of fraud and numerous other illegal activities. Though he was not directly involved in those activities, he emerged with the strong taint of association. Sometimes he blamed himself for not being more aware of what was going on, instead of being a happy cog in the corporate wheel who made money and spent most of it. When he tried to reestablish himself and sought work with American companies, the corporate grapevine preceded him, and he was shut out. He lived on dwindling investments and occasional projects as a consulting petroleum market analyst. His recent move to this small apartment further out of the city was a necessary economy.

As he continued to scratch his furry friend, Jamal thought about the surgery for Scheherazade. At first, he didn't know how he could come up with $2,500. Then he looked at the only remaining item from his successful corporate rise. Next to Scheherazade, the Ferrari gave him the most pleasure and reminded him of better times.

"Jamal," he had told himself, "you are a sentimental fool. Sell the Ferrari and get something sensible, unattractive to vandals. A car that drinks less gasoline. Then you will have the money you need." Now even that would not help.

Jamal finished his drink and went into the kitchen. He warmed a frozen dinner in the microwave but had no idea what he was eating. His thoughts were for Zadie. He had not realized the depth of his attachment to her until Dr. Norris first described the condition of her left eye and the impending blindness. Then the doctor raised Jamal's hope with the suggestion of surgery, only to tell him today that it was not possible. The idea of Zadie enduring total blindness was unthinkable. She would never be able to run and chase through the nearby park. Zadie would be afraid of the darkness no matter what Dr. Norris said.

"I know Zadie best," he murmured, feeling the tears form in the corners of his eyes. He let them roll down his cheeks. His barely touched dinner sat on the countertop.

Jamal made himself another drink and returned to his chair where the two sat before a dark television. The little dog seemed to absorb Jamal's despair and snuggled as close as possible.

"What to do, Zadie?"

She looked up at him but didn't wag her tail. They sat until time to go to bed.

Jamal put on his pajamas and Scheherazade curled up in her bed which lay on the floor next to his bed. Jamal went into the bathroom and returned with an armful of towels. He rolled one into a stick and placed it on the window sill, tight against the window's bottom edge and pulled the drape. He did the same thing at the window in the living room and at the bottom of the front door. In the kitchen, he extinguished the pilot light and turned on each burner as far as possible. There was a faint hiss, then silence.

Jamal sat on the edge of the bed and looked down at Scheherazade who lay on her bed. Large, round brown eyes fixed on his. He reached down to scratch her and was amazed to see a tear fall from each eye. She wagged her tail slowly, nuzzled her nose in his hand. Jamal heard a soft whimper.

"How could you know, Zadie?"

He sprang from the bed, dashed across the hall into the kitchen and quickly turned off the burners and relit the pilot light. Returning to the bedroom, Jamal lay down, his hand reaching down to softly scratch his dog.

"Jamal, you are not only a fool, you are an idiot, first class."

A Shove Out of the Nest

"Hi, Daddy. It's Jennifer."

"Hi, honey. It's good to hear your voice."

"I know it's been a while, and I'm truly sorry I don't call more often. But you remember what college is like. So many things to do and not enough time. This last quarter has been a bear."

"Tell me about it." Dad chuckled.

"Well, I had to drop Economics and American History because the assignments were piling up, and my other classes were falling too."

"So, that leaves you with?"

"Contemporary Life Decisions and Acrylic Art in the Abstract. Oh, and I'm on the Gamma Gamma Gamma soccer team now which means practice every afternoon. That really wipes me out."

"I can imagine."

"How are you and Mom doing?"

"We're doing just fine. Now that I've retired—"

"That's great. You and Mom are the best. I really miss you."

"Well, I—"

"One reason I called is that I have a problem, and I hope you can help me."

"Is it money, Jen?"

"Well, yes. How did you know?"

"The last time you had a problem—"

"Yes, and I really appreciated your coming to my rescue. I don't know why these things happen to me, but all of a sudden, my Visa card is maxed. Honestly, I'm so embarrassed. But if you could—"

"Jennifer, you're not supposed to have a Visa card. Or any other kind of credit card. Not after the last time."

"Well, I got this wonderful offer on email with no interest for the first three months."

"What's the interest now?"

"Can you believe eighteen percent, and they didn't bother to let me know until I missed a payment last month? I guess I never got the notice on email, but today the notification came and there were extra charges, added to the current purchases. Now I'm over the limit. Wow! I couldn't believe it."

"How much?"

"Uh, let me check. Just $5,145. That's everything. Oh, Popsy, I'm so sorry." There was a hint of tearing up.

"Jennifer, do you realize that's almost twice what you were in for the last time? Barely a year ago? How do you do that, girl? I thought you'd learned your lesson. You promised your mother and me—"

"Please Father, I don't need a sermon. I'm truly sick about this. I didn't set out to do it deliberately. I'm not that kind of person." There was a pause. "I'm your daughter," she wailed.

"Yes, and since I'm your father, this is what we're going to do. You are going to go to the registrar's office tomorrow and find out what you can get a degree in after four and a half years. I'll give you two more quarters. But no more Gamma Gamma Gamma. I'll be there in a couple of days and we're going to the Credit Counseling Service so they can develop a plan for you to pay off your bills. Don't be surprised if it takes a while. Oh, yes. You're going to need a job. And, destroy that card immediately. Don't even think about another one. Ever."

"Oh, Daddy."

"We love you too, sweetheart."

Mary's Ring

"Ich liebe dich, Mary." My grandmother smiled as she repeated the words my grandfather whispered on their wedding day in May 1900. "My name is Annie Mary, but he always called me Mary." She spoke with a strong German accent.

"On his grave marker, Grandpa's name is Adolph Gus. What did you call him?" I asked.

"At first he was Adolph. After we had nine children, he became Papa to me too. He was a good Papa and a faithful husband." Small, fragile Grandma sat hunched in her wheelchair. Since I could remember, my grandmother had worn her gray hair pulled into a small knot on the nape of her neck. Dentures stretched her lips into a straight line. Her eyes still sparkled, however, and she chuckled frequently.

"I've never heard how you and Grandpa met," I said.

"My folks sent me out to work when I was sixteen. We were very poor, and the farm barely supported our family. I worked for Mrs. Baker whose husband had a large farm. I cleaned house, cooked and tended a vegetable garden. There were six children. Their oldest, Mary, took care of her mother who was in poor health." She paused in remembering. "Your grandpa came to work for Mr. Baker as the foreman when he was twenty-eight. I was twenty-three by then. We worked hard."

"Grandpa was a good looking young man. I would have fallen for him in a minute."

"Yah," she chuckled. "You probably would. With thick blonde hair and a full mustache, he was handsome and strong. He wasn't a tall man, but oh my, how he walked—his back straight and long strides. You could tell he was a man of determination. I realized he was good husband material the first time I saw him."

"I bet Grandpa had his eye on you too."

"No. That took longer. Your grandpa fell in love with Mary Baker. She was seventeen or eighteen, very pretty and a nice girl. Your grandpa started courting her. I'd see them holding hands while swinging on the front porch. One evening I saw them kiss."

"Weren't you jealous? Didn't you try to flirt so he would notice?"

"I guess I was jealous, but in those days, you knew your place and I didn't want to lose my job." She smiled. "But I wasn't so dumb either."

"What do you mean?"

"I cooked and served breakfast, dinner and supper for the Bakers and the workers. Your grandpa and the men ate in the kitchen. I always made sure he got the best servings and the largest piece of pie or cake. He didn't seem to notice, but I didn't give up."

"What was Grandpa really like? I wish I had known him better, but we always lived far away and he died when I was ten."

"You would have gotten along very well. I remember the first night he had supper at the farm. He was quiet and dignified. I thought it was because he would be boss the next morning. The men were leery of him because of his German accent, but it wasn't too long before they learned to work together. Mr. Baker always said your grandpa got more work out of them than anyone else he'd ever hired. Before long they were laughing and talking at meal times and telling dirty stories when they thought I couldn't hear. Well, not too dirty. Your grandpa wasn't one of the storytellers, but I heard him laugh." Grandma smiled.

"How long was it before Grandpa noticed you?"

"When your grandpa asked for Mary's hand in marriage, Mr. Baker said he didn't want his daughter to marry an immigrant, especially one who didn't own a farm. It didn't matter that your grandpa was saving his money to buy a place. Mr. Baker decided Mary would marry a neighboring farmer who had a farm larger than his. Mr. Allen was a widower with three young children. He was a fine-looking man, but not as handsome as your grandpa. He was older too."

"Poor Mary. I wouldn't have wanted to grow up in those days."

"She didn't seem upset by it. I think she looked forward to having her own home that was nicer than her mother's."

"How did Grandpa take it?"

"I thought he might leave, but the money was good, jobs were scarce. He was hoping to buy a farm as soon as he had enough money. One day I was weeding and thinning the garden when he came by and stopped to talk with me."

"I can see you now, kneeling in the dirt, hands grimy and probably sweat on your face in that hot Texas sun. Do you remember what he said?"

"Of course, I do. 'Miss Mary, what are you growing in there?' Not very romantic, but he noticed me. Afterward, we talked at meal times and in the garden. I was German too, so we talked in "plat Deutsch," low German. Some of the men teased us, but he smiled and soon I did too."

"Did it take Grandpa long to get over Mary Baker?"

"It seemed like a long time to me, but we became good friends rather soon. He even showed me the gold wedding band he had bought for her with Mary and Adolph engraved in it."

I didn't ask to see the inside of the gold band she wore on her left hand.

All's Fair in Love and Cooking

Patsy Bailey came home from her job at the library madder than a wet hen. Jane Wilson had been her friend a long time, but today she went too far.

"Oh, Patsy," Jane said, "I want that recipe for the wonderful French spiced chicken you brought to the church potluck last month. I didn't eat any, but everyone said it was the best thing they'd ever tasted. Even Fred Haskell." Since Fred Haskell came to Bloomfield, there was a gleam in Jane's eye. Old maid schoolteacher, Patsy thought. Won't she ever give up?

Jane's request surprised Patsy because Jane cooked as little as possible. She always said, "Anybody can cook," meaning that being a schoolteacher was harder and more important. Patsy admired Jane for being a teacher. It wasn't easy, but cooking took imagination as well as brains. One day when Jane said, "Anybody can cook," Patsy handed her a cookbook. "Then, why don't you?" Jane harrumphed and stalked out of the library. Today, she was sweet as you please.

"Why do you want to make French spiced chicken?" Patsy asked.

"Fred Haskell is coming to dinner at my house this Saturday."

Patsy felt like slapping the self-satisfied expression off Jane's face but was sweet as you please right back.

"I didn't know you and Fred Haskell were friends."

"Oh, yes," she gushed. "Fred was at the store talking to Leroy about some tools when I was there yesterday," Jane said. "We got to talking, and before I knew it he was coming to dinner."

Leroy is Jane's brother. He's a real sourpuss. No wonder his wife left him all those years ago. Now Leroy and Jane live in the old Wilson house, and Leroy runs the family hardware store.

"I'll pick up the recipe tomorrow." Jane flounced out of the library without waiting for Patsy to say yes or no. That riled Patsy.

Patsy lives alone and likes it that way, though when she saw Fred Haskell in church and learned he was unmarried, she thought about things. She was engaged to Roland Gates when he left to serve in World War II. He was killed in the Solomon Islands. An only child, Patsy stayed in the family home. She drifted into the job at the library, and nothing better came along—until maybe Fred Haskell.

Through the years, Patsy and Jane were close friends who nagged and found fault with one another much like a long-married couple. Patsy resented Jane's criticism of her hair being pulled into a bun, saying it made her look like a librarian. Patsy came back at Jane, saying she didn't have the legs for the short skirts she wore. On and on.

Patsy spoke to Fred Haskell several times at church, and he came to the library every week. He was round-faced, beginning to bald, sported a slight paunch, nice and gentle spoken. He always checked out a stack of books, including cookbooks. Once he told Patsy about a Julia Child dish he'd made. At the time, Patsy thought it might be nice to have a husband who liked to cook.

The next day Jane came to the library after school.

"Patsy, I hope you remembered to bring that recipe. I looked for it in some cookbooks but didn't find it."

"That's because it's one I developed myself." Patsy wasn't lying. She'd seen a simple recipe for baked chicken and experimented. Some versions weren't so good, but finally, she created a savory recipe using fresh rosemary and dry sherry. You couldn't taste those ingredients, but it definitely made the dish.

"Are you going to be one of those people who won't share a good recipe?" Jane demanded.

"No. I have it right here." Patsy handed Jane a 3x5 card, neatly typed. The ingredients were on one side, except for the rosemary and sherry. The directions on the reverse failed to mention skinning the chicken. Under Jane's hand, the dish would be bland and swim in fat. Patsy felt sorry for Fred Haskell, but all's fair in love and cooking.

What's in a Word?

Solving crossword puzzles diluted the dreary reality of Lily's days. This afternoon she needed a four-letter word for soapstone. Since she wasn't sure what soapstone was or might mean, she reached for the telephone, pushed the numbers she knew by heart and helped herself to a chocolate truffle from the gold and blue box on the table next to her chaise.

"Claudine? You gotta minute? I'm stuck on the crossword. I wonder if you'd mind looking it up in the big dictionary?"

Claudine was the dispatcher at Armond, Louisiana Police Station, as well as in charge of the town's two hundred volume library, housed in a former weapons closet. Lenier Parish Library System supplied new books every six months plus a permanent deposit of five basic references which included an unabridged dictionary. Lily was allowed one call a day to solve the crossword puzzle in New Orleans' *The Times-Picayune*. Many days she didn't need her allocation.

"What is it this time?" Snappish. "I'm busy, you know."

Likes to make you feel beholden, thought Lily. Also lies a lot. Busy!

"Oh, Claudine, you are so kind to help me. Soapstone." She spelled it slowly. Claudine insisted on that. "I need a four-letter word, please and thank you."

Insincere, syrupy. Lily smiled with satisfaction knowing it got Claudine's goat every time. She probably has some four-letter words on the tip of her tongue, thought Lily.

"I'll hafta call you back."

Claudine banged the telephone into its cradle but Lily was holding the receiver away from her ear. She hung up, reached for a truffle and tackled the next word. An hour and a half later, the telephone rang.

"The dictionary says, 'Soapstone, a soft stone having a soapy feel and composed essentially of talc, chlorite and often some magnetite. Compare steatite,' which says, 'a massive talc having a grayish green or brown color and forming extensive beds.' The word you want is talc, t-a-l-c." Claudine banged the telephone into its cradle.

Lily had already hung up soundlessly on "grayish," and reached for another truffle.

Beyond Reach

The gray-haired woman placed her easel on the knoll above a chattering stream that flowed over rocks. Drooping tree branches scattered shards of sunlight over sudden drifts of shadow. She breathed the clean air deeply, feeling its caress. So many days she trudged from an old house on the hill through the lea, into woods to sit in this place and put her message on canvas.

She sat on a smooth flat rock before a small easel that held her work in progress. She daubed a spatula into a box of paints and placed colors onto a stained palette. Beside her, a small pistol lay in the grass.

She placed her brush on the canvas beside the trunk of a tree she had painted. Its green branches hung over blue, frothy streaks like the water flowing below. She moved the brush to the other side of the stream where she painted large gray rocks, cushioning them in long green grass, forming a steep bank. To complete the top of the canvas, she painted lower trunks of tall trees, seemingly held together by thick growing brush. A few streaks of sunshine highlighted random trunks.

The woman paused in her work, looking closely at the flowing water depicted on her canvas. A small space mid creek was unpainted. She sat for some time looking at the scene before her and then at her unfinished work. She chose different brushes and daubed fresh paint on the palette. Painstakingly, she filled the empty spot, studying her left hand as she reached up, copying it onto the canvas into the middle of the stream. After a few more strokes, she cleaned the brushes and palette, closed the paint container and placed them in a basket that she tossed into the creek, where it sank.

Reaching into her sweater pocket, she took out a small picture, yellowed and fading. In another time, she stood beside a tall young man who wore a khaki uniform and overseas' cap. She put it back in her pocket, picked up the small weapon and checked that it contained a shot. Standing at the creek's edge with her back to the water, she placed the pistol to her temple and pulled the trigger. As she'd planned, her body fell backward into the deep stream. A hand reached upward as water closed around her.

Callie

When Grandma said, "Now what?" I knew something was wrong and raised up from the row of carrots I was thinning. Perspiration trickled from beneath my straw hat and rolled into my ears. Grandma stood, shading her eyes as she peered through the dusty haze hovering over the pasture land. I saw a blue and silver transcontinental bus pull away, revealing a woman who crossed the highway. She began trudging down the rutted dirt track leading to our house.

"Is that Mama?" I whispered. Grandma didn't answer. The woman's chin rested on her chest so that I saw only the top of her head. Each step seemed an effort. A large suitcase in one hand and a smaller one in the other tugged at her shoulders. I was afraid she might fall any minute.

"Mama, Mama!" I jumped over the low picket fence surrounding the garden and ran toward the struggling figure. As I got closer, I saw that her once luxuriant hair was dull and stringy. She wore a cheap cotton print dress and flat sandals. When she looked up and saw me, she tried to smile, but her lips dissolved into a grimace and tears ran down her cheeks. Her beautiful face was pale and drawn. I wanted to cry too, but Mama was crying enough for both of us.

The last time we'd seen Mama, almost two years ago, she'd come driving up in a shiny, black Model A Ford, dressed to kill and accompanied by a self-important, rotund man wearing a tan plaid suit and brown derby. She introduced Mr. Paul Apton as her new husband. "He's in banking," Mama said. They stayed for dinner and said they had to be in Waco for the night. In my journal, dated May 13, 1928, I called him Mr. P.A. as in Pompous Ass. Unfortunately, I was right.

When I was seven, my daddy was killed working on an oil rig in East Texas. Soon after, Mama moved us from the little house with the big green yard to one room in Mrs. Raddler's boarding house. We had the clothes on our backs and my dearest possessions: Goldie, the baby doll I couldn't remember not having, and a book with Mother Goose on the cover. When the money from the oil company was gone, Mama decided to go to Houston and look for work.

"I can't take you with me until I find a job and get settled. Grandma Lila says she'd like to have you come and stay with her awhile."

I kind of remembered a time long ago when we went to see Grandma, who lived on a farm. I also remembered Mama yelling and crying. I didn't remember much about Grandma except she hugged me a lot.

"It'll be a nice time for you and Grandma Lila to get to know one another," Mama said.

Grandma's farm was five miles out of Duddley, Texas, about a hundred miles west of Houston. Grandma and her husband, Jack Graham, farmed until he was found dead in the south field. Heart attack. Now Grandma leased out all but the ten acres where she had her house, small garden, a barn with chickens and two cows. A couple of live oak trees shaded the house and yard.

"Gives me breathing room and the means to feed myself," Grandma explained when I asked why she lived there. Grandma didn't have a lot to say, but I liked being around her. She taught me to cook and how to keep the house clean. I learned to feed the chickens and collect the eggs. It took a while before I could bring myself to chop off a chicken's head, pluck the feathers, cook and eat it. I was good at milking the cows. The best part was working in the vegetable garden and taking care of all the flowers in her yard. I felt safe for the first time since my daddy died.

Grandma liked to read, and we made regular trips to the library. Toward the end of summer, Mama wrote to say it wouldn't be convenient for me to stay with her during the school year. "It's very convenient for me," Grandma said and gave me a hug. She told me she planned to take me to school the first day. I was in fifth grade and said I could ride the bus.

"It's a new school, Callie, and I want them to know your grandmother is as interested in your school work as any other parent. It will make a difference." She didn't say, "Since your mother doesn't seem to care." That afternoon she was at the highway to meet the school bus. Grandma helped me with my homework that evening and every evening after dinner. I liked school for the first time.

After Mama and Mr. P.A. showed up that one time, almost two years passed during which we heard from Mama regularly. Her letters didn't say a lot, but she seemed happy. The postmarks were from different places in Texas, Oklahoma and Louisiana. One thing bothered me. Mama would write she was coming for a visit, but something always happened. When the letters got shorter and then we didn't hear anything for six months, I began to worry.

"Try not to worry, Callie. Your mama has a way of landing on her feet."

When the transcontinental bus stopped in front of Grandma's farm, our wondering was laid to rest. I couldn't believe how broken my mother looked. I loosened her fingers from the suitcases. They plopped to the ground in a puff of dust. Mama tottered, and I wrapped my arms around her. Running toward her I'd seen how the dress pulled tight across her rounded stomach. I hugged her carefully.

Grandma came up and put her arms around both of us.

Checking Out

I'd been standing in line for some time at the supermarket, waiting to check out, when I heard a faint sob behind me. I decided not to turn around, fearing to intrude on someone's private moment. Besides, it could have been a sigh or gulp for air. Mind your own business, I told myself.

The store was crowded with late evening shoppers. I supposed many were, like me, on the way home from work and trying to squeeze in one more weekly chore before facing the nightly routine of dinner, homework, refereeing, trying to be organized. Ha! My basket was piled high as was the one ahead of me. However, they were nearly finished, and my long wait would be over.

Again, I heard the sound. Louder this time. Longer. I still didn't look. Then I felt a firm bump to my posterior from the basket behind. Surprise caused me to turn around. A young woman looked at me with one eye. She held a tissue to the other.

"Oh, did I bump you?" she asked in a halting, whispery voice. "I'm so sorry." She half smiled, but I had the feeling she knew darn well she'd pushed me—not so slightly.

I smiled to let her know there was no harm done. Before I could turn around, she gave a long deep gasp and covered both eyes with the tissue. Her shoulders shook.

"Are you okay?" I asked.

She began to hiccup in between the sobs, then suddenly uncovered her eyes. "I'm sorry to be such a mess, but everything has gone wrong today, and now I'll be late getting home. He never understands." More sobs.

I looked at her more carefully. Her eyes weren't puffy in spite of the crying. She wore a long-sleeved, gray sweatshirt, a bit tatty and soiled. Her long, brassy blonde hair was tatty and dirty too. She became more agitated and kept looking at her watch.

With mixed feelings, I said to her, "Why don't you go in front of me? The woman ahead is about finished. I'm not in a hurry." What a fat lie, but I had visions of this stressed creature going home to some lout, lounging at the kitchen table, consuming number six of a six-pack. I imagined the sarcasm, intimidation, probably salted with foul language. At least that wasn't waiting for me.

Her face broke into happiness and relief. I was afraid she was going to wrap me in the arms of that sweatshirt. Instead, we changed places just as the checker got ready for his next customer. I noticed two six-packs of beer in her cart.

It was getting dark, but I knew where my car was parked. As I approached, I saw the blonde woman stuffing bags into the back of a dirty, elderly van parked next to me. She stepped to the other side of the vehicle and got in. As I unloaded my groceries, I heard voices through the van's open window. The woman talked loudly to a man, laughing and saying, "Yeah, it worked again. I put on my tearful, abused look, hiccupped and sobbed. I had to use the basket to get her attention, but she fell for it. Probably is congratulating herself on saving me from my nightly abuse." Loud laughter from both of them and the pop of two drink cans being opened.

I don't know what possessed me, but I quickly reached down to the almost treadless rear tire of the van and disengaged the valve stem. Sitting in my car, hiding my face with the newspaper, I waited until they chugged out of the parking lot into the heavy traffic. I followed for several miles of stop and go. Sure enough, the rear tire went flat. After they were able to pull to the side of the street, I passed and gave them a blast from my horn. Then I got on my cell phone and reported the location of two people driving and consuming beer.

The Escape

"How long before we get to Hawkinsville, lawman?"

"Day after tomorrow."

"That long?"

"What's your hurry? That jail cell is small and hot this time of year."

"Oh, I don't figure your jail'll hold me for long. Probably not as long as last time." He smiled. "What was it? A week?"

"We're ready for you this time. After the circuit judge gets around to you, we'll be fixing your noose and getting the trap door ready."

"Maybe. Gimme some more of them beans and a cup of that swill you call coffee."

"Mind your mouth. You're lucky Jim Massie didn't come for you. You can't rile me like you do him,"

"Well, now. Why would I wanna do that?"

"Just shut up and eat. We'll make camp on the Guadalupe tonight. Be a lot cooler."

"Ain't you the considerate one? You know, I been thinking if I oughta tell you something. Something you don't know."

"Just shut up and finish your grub."

"And since you're being so kind to me, I think I will make you a wiser man."

"Don't do me any favors. It took me two weeks to find you in Juarez and get you back across the Rio Grande. One day on the trail, and I'm sick and tired of listening to you. I'm not interested in anything you have to say."

"We're a little techy, ain't we?" But I'm gonna tell you anyway." He pauses. "I knew your Kate before you ever came along."

"I told you to shut up!"

"Pretty girl in those days. Beautiful woman now. Even after all them babies you give her."

"I'm warning you, shut up!"

"It was in Fayette where her no-account daddy left her mama and all them kids. Kate being the oldest had to bring in money to take care of them. That's where I met her, working in The White Horse."

"Carson, you never knew her or anybody like her. She wouldn't give you the time of day."

"No. But the time of night, that's different. Imagine my surprise. Meeting her again in Hawkinsville after all these years. Same old Kate. She had no trouble remembering me. Just like old times. You sure get called out of the county a lot, don't you?"

"I'm telling you, Shut up!"

"I was just thinking, lawman. If you was to let me go ... escape ... I wouldn't be going to Hawkinsville ever again. Never see nobody who'd be interested in Kate, saloon girl, wife of John Durbin, deputy sheriff of Lamosa County. Or Kate's old jailbird friend, Frank Carson. Be a lot easier for all of us."

"Carson, you're not only a murderer, cattle rustler, thief. You're a liar and scum of the earth. I hope that judge says, 'Hang him high.'"

"When I get to talking to that judge, I'll have lots to tell him. It may be that I'll remember how that nice Miz Durbin helped me get out of jail."

"Carson, I'm beginning to think you really would do something like that."

Carson raised an eyebrow and smiled.

Durbin took the cuffs off. "If I ever lay eyes on you again ..."

"I'll be damned. You gonna let me go ain't you? On my horse?

"No horse, just your canteen. Start running back the way we came. That's more than you deserve."

"Juarez, here I come. Tell Kate goodbye for me."

Carson turned and started running.

Durbin shot him. "You shoulda' shut up the first time."

Joel

"They must have names," Joel said, watching the afternoon light slant through a glass aquarium where three goldfish swam in lazy circles, diving elegantly, colors flashing. The boy burst out laughing whenever they glided through a ceramic castle and mock seaweed fronds. "I christen you Mr. Hat, Cowboy, and Miss Plume."

"How did you come up with those names?" Marta asked, brushing a lock of hair from Joel's brow. He shook his head and it fell back across his forehead.

"Look at them, Mama." Joel pointed to the white spot on the head of the largest. A black patch resembling a saddle extended from side to side of the plumpest. A pale, golden, longish fish shimmered with each movement of its plume-like tail. "Don't you see?" I think Papa will like Cowboy best."

Marta smiled at her son's enjoyment.

The boy gazed as the fish swam around the large bowl. "Do you think Papa will come to see me soon?"

Marta took a breath. "He is very busy, but I'm sure he will."

"When I am better, we must go to America to see him."

"Perhaps." Joel's mother moved to the kitchen, dabbing her eyes with her apron. The boy did not notice.

One morning, on their outing through the neighborhood, Marta and Joel had noticed a large aquarium filled with goldfish in the window of Madame Clambert's Shoppe. This was new, and Joel insisted they go in. Marta could not refuse him. He chose thoughtfully and now enjoyed their enthusiastic performance.

Joel fed them every day. "Not too much," Marta taught him, "or they will sicken and die."

Joel wanted to care for the fish as Madame had instructed, but Marta explained that his arms and hands weren't strong enough to lift the aquarium or to manage the cleaning and refilling. Disappointment turned to satisfaction when he learned to scoop with a small net, transferring them to a large bowl of water. Marta curbed her impulse to steady the pale hand. Joel watched as his mother cleaned the aquarium, the castle and the seaweed.

"Mama, I believe you missed something inside the castle." Marta smiled and cleaned it once more.

One day after Joel returned his fish to their clean home, he tapped on the side of the bowl. The fish responded with excited dives and swirls through the castle and seaweed. Joel laughed until deep racking coughs took away his breath. Marta wheeled his chair into the bathroom, turned on hot water in the shower for steam, and gave him a spoonful of dark syrup.

"Breathe slowly," she calmed the shivering little boy. When his breathing became regular, Marta settled him into bed and sang softly until he fell asleep. Her lips brushed his curls as she willed her heart to beat more slowly.

One day, Joel insisted they take the fish to the park.

"The fresh air and sunshine are good for me, so it will be good for them."

Joel sat in his wheelchair while his mother placed a clear plastic container, smaller than the aquarium, on his lap. A lid with small holes kept the fish and splashes inside. Joel held the container with both hands, murmuring assurances as Marta pushed his chair across cobblestone streets and along paths in the nearby park. Other walkers noticed the frail boy's contented smile beneath tousled black curls that matched the young woman's. They could only guess at what the lap robe concealed.

After lessons were finished, Joel sat at the table many hours. He sang to the fish. He read to them from his favorite books. He tapped on the side of the bowl and called their names. The fish swam over, their mouths opening and closing.

"Mama. They talk to me. They say they are glad I brought them to live with us." His laughter echoed throughout the small rooms.

Marta sits with clasped hands stretched across the table, not feeling the warmth of the sun. Tangled graying ringlets fall on slumped shoulders. Her eyes see nothing. She hears a small splash and turns to see Mr. Hat, Cowboy and Miss Plume gathered at the side of the aquarium, gaping. Marta stares at them for a moment before picking up the box of fish food. There is a long pause as the fish continue to open and close their mouths. She takes the box, begins tipping it over the bowl. "Not too much," she whispers.

"Daisy, come quick. He's back." The small, shaggy-bearded man danced a few steps in excitement.

A woman moved her girth sideways through the screen door. Frizzy dark-rooted blond hair framed her splotchy, sagging face. She snatched the binoculars and trained them on a distant stand of trees growing across Cape Falcon.

"Yeah, Jess, he's somethin' all right," she grunted.

"He's the biggest I ever seen." A toothless grin spread across his face.

Baltasharm, after circling twice, landed beside the spacious nest resting in limbs high atop a fir tree snag where Amaturelle sat keeping three eggs warm. This was not her idea of fun, but she always took good care of her brood.

"Those creatures are looking our way again," Baltasharm said.

Amaturelle peered toward the cabin tucked into the hillside cove.

"They're pointing," she said. "How rude."

"What a wretched looking creature."

"Which one?" Amaturelle giggled.

"You're right. They both look unappetizing."

"The small one is so bony. I wonder if the round one eats most of their catch?"

Baltasharm peered down at two creatures standing on the deck of the cabin. They had been there two days, looking and pointing toward the nest. The eagle was concerned because he'd seen similar creatures take what looked like a small tree limb, from which all growth had been stripped, and point it skyward. After a loud noise, a bird fell from the sky, never to fly again. The creatures seemed to prefer ducks, but last year Baltasharm saw a friend eagle fall and watched the creatures carry it away. One had to be careful.

"I wish they would go away," Amaturelle said.

"These seem harmless," said Baltasharm. "I don't see a tree limb, but I would like to know what they are holding up to their faces when they look toward us."

"Oh, Baltasharm, you know about so many things. I feel safe when you are near."

Baltasharm, stretched to his full height and breadth, lifted from the tree and took to the air. Circling the nest, he dipped his wings in a salute to Amaturelle and soared out over the ocean. She knew dinner was on the way.

"Look at him, Daisy. Have you ever seen such a sight? Wish I could fly like that."

"Good grief, Jess, how can you get so excited over a bird? You, fly? Get your skinny butt in the house. We're having Spam for dinner."

Daisy went inside. Jess sighed and followed.

It was twilight when Baltasharm flew toward the nest. Jess grabbed the binoculars.

"Holy cow! What's he got? Daisy, come look."

There was no answer, only the blare of a television. Jess watched as the eagle circled, holding what looked like a large fish in his talons. Baltasharm swooped in and laid it carefully on the nest so that it hung evenly over the sides. He waited for Amaturelle to take the first bite before tearing away a large piece.

"Them birds are somethin' else."

Jess kept watch during the next week. One evening before sunset, he raised the binoculars. Baltasharm sat on a snag next to the one where Amaturelle had nested all day. Amaturelle turned to Baltasharm, spread her wings, and lifted off into the glowing sky. Baltasharm moved to the nest and settled over the eggs.

"Dang me. I never seen such a sight."

Jess followed Amaturelle until she flew toward the sun and he lost sight of her. Before long, he saw her circling the trees and dipping low over the waves. She swooped past the nest several times. In a slow approach, Amaturelle settled beside Baltasharm and rubbed her beak against his.

"Them birds," Jess whispered, "I wouldn't believe it if I didn't see it with my own eyes."

The screen door opened and slapped shut.

"Still watching them birds?" Daisy snapped.

Jess didn't reply as he continued to watch the nest.

"I was thinking that big one would make a mighty nice stuffed trophy," she said. "Get us some money."

"Daisy, you know I'm outta that kinda stuff. Besides with that last conviction, I cain't have no guns on the place. They'd put me away 'til kingdom come."

"My brother Moody's got a powerful rifle with a scope and everything. He could drop it right off that snag onto the ground. He's a good shot."

"I don't want him around. Moody means trouble. He's the one shoulda gone to jail." Jess went into the cabin, letting the door slam.

"Baltasharm, I think the little ones are almost ready. I hear faint tapping."

"I hope you're right. We'll be busier than ever, but I always look forward to the time we have before they leave."

"Me too. They're so helpless at first." Amaturelle sighed.

"And hungry." Baltasharm chuckled. "But they strengthen quickly and are gone."

Three days later two eggs cracked open, and two little eaglets began their constant demand for something to eat. The third egg became silent and never opened. Baltasharm removed it with his beak. This had happened before, but their sorrow was short lived. The parents were busy and happy with the two who cheeped constantly. Baltasharm was a good provider and brought home all kinds of good eating for his family. They took turns dropping the niblets into the open beaks so that Amaturelle could fly out and refresh herself. At night Baltasharm perched close by.

"It's time to name them," Baltasharm announced when they were two days old.

"I like Litarianne for our daughter," said Amaturelle.

"I think our son should be called Samatobis. What do you think?" asked Baltasharm.

"Perfect names for perfect children," their mother said, grooming the little ones.

"They will do well." Their father tapped each little head with his beak.

Baltasharm looked out over the water and observed the sun setting toward a clear horizon. Streaks of pink stretched across the graying sky. He turned his gaze to the creatures on the cabin deck. There were three this time. The new one had a dark head with green and blue on his body. He was taller than the others. Baltasharm gasped as the large creature raised a tree limb to his shoulder and put his face down to a small box attached to it. He pointed it toward the nest, but the bony creature pushed it down.

"Amaturelle! Cover the little ones and press down into the nest as deeply as possible. Do not look up."

Amaturelle obeyed Baltasharm. When he gave terse orders, something terrible was about to happen. Though her head was tucked under a wing, she was aware that her mate moved about on nearby limbs. The little ones huddled against their mother and were quiet.

"Stay as you are. I'm going to fly out over the ocean into the sun. When he points the limb toward me, the bright rays will blind him. I will return when they cannot see me."

"I love you, Baltasharm." A rush of wind under strong wings was the only reply.

Moments later a loud noise made her heart beat as though it would tear open her feathered breast. The following silence terrified her. Amaturelle imagined the worst: She would never see Baltasharm again.

After a while, Amaturelle, head down, huddling over her babies, heard the familiar sound of circling wings. Baltasharm landed on the edge of the nest and smoothed Amaturelle's feathers with his beak.

"Baltasharm!" she cried, looking up at him, searching for a wound.

"I am safe and whole, dear one. I believe we have a guardian spirit."

"What do you mean, my love?"

"As I lifted into the air, I heard a loud noise. Like the one I told you about."

"Yes, I heard it too." Amaturelle shivered with the memory.

"I felt no impact and expected another loud noise because I'd not reached the sun's protection. When none came, I circled the creatures' nest and saw the small one pulling the tree limb from the large one. He threw it into the water below. The large one began lashing out. The round one tried to grab him. He swung out and knocked her to the floor of the nest. They rolled about, screeching and calling like a flock of crows."

"Oh, Baltasharm."

"The tree limb fell into those rocks where the ocean pounds day and night. We are safe for now."

The Exchange

I gave him my telephone number the night we met.

Guests sat on the lanai drinking cocktails and munching assorted hors d'oeuvres. Ukuleles strummed softly out of sight. An erratic breeze moved tall palms. My flowered, silk dress was comfortable in the tropical evening.

When I saw him approaching, I noticed that he wore a navy blazer over a white polo shirt and white linen slacks. He also stepped on my foot when he reached the bench where I sat. His apology sounded sincere but practiced. I wondered later how many times he had offered it.

"Promise you won't tell a soul what a tangle foot I am," he pleaded with a smile. "I can do better if you give me the chance." He spoke with a faint accent I couldn't identify.

How could I refuse? I was more disconcerted than he, and not because I was in pain. At that moment, he could have stomped both my feet so long as he kept smiling. This was the most handsome man I had ever seen off the movie screen, and he was smiling, asking to sit beside me.

"I don't recall seeing you before. Do you live on Oahu or one of the other islands?" he asked.

"Neither. I live in Kansas. I'm visiting my sister who lives at Schofield Barracks, where her husband is stationed. They're here, somewhere."

When I asked where he lived, he hesitated, then said, "I travel a good deal but this is where I live whenever I can." I thought about that later, too.

I wondered where he traveled and what he did for a living, because his clothes were expensive, as was the elegant watch he wore. Later, I realized that he hadn't told me much about himself but had discovered a lot about me. I am still embarrassed remembering how much I talked about myself. It amazed me at how everything I said fell on rapt ears. He sat close and took one of my hands, holding it gently. A waiter brought us fresh drinks.

It was wonderful how he devoted himself to me. Ordinarily, such an attractive man would have sought someone not so plain. He didn't seem to know anyone else, and no one came over to speak to either of us. I noticed other women, some very pretty, looking at us from time to time. My vanity soared and I decided to enjoy my good luck.

As we walked through the extensive garden, he glanced at his watch and seemed surprised at the hour.

"It's later than I thought. I'm afraid I must say 'aloha' and hope we meet again. Perhaps you would give me your phone number?" His smile disarmed me.

Without hesitation, I agreed but had nothing on which to write. He went through his pockets with no luck, when seemingly out of nowhere there appeared a white-coated manservant. My friend asked him, whom I took to be Japanese, if he could get us a bit of paper. Reaching into the pocket of his serving jacket, the small man handed him a notepad and pen.

As I wrote my name and number, I happened to see my handsome friend surreptitiously pass a letter sized leather pouch to the servant who quickly put it inside his jacket. Since I wasn't supposed to see the transaction, nor did I want to spoil the new friendship, I said nothing.

We parted with a polite embrace and the soft touch of his lips to my cheek.

The Japanese bombed Pearl Harbor the next morning.

He never called.

Brother Ralph

Mama and I were weeding the vegetable garden. Sweat crawled over my skin and a tingling itch crept up my nose, but I had something else on my mind.

"Mama?"

"Yes?"

"I'd like to go to the Sunshine Club at church."

Mama sat back on her heels and frowned.

Brother Ralph, the preacher, had done something bad to her. I didn't know what it was, but since then we didn't go to church, and Mama wasn't herself. Noises bothered her at night, and one day I saw her crying when she was taking sheets from the clothesline. I tried to be good and prayed every night that God would send Brother Ralph far, far away.

Mama continued frowning, and I knew she was wondering why I wanted to go to anything at the preacher's church.

"What brought this on?" Her voice rose a bit.

If I'd told her my real reason, she'd have forbidden it.

"Doris Watson asked me to go with her. It's for fifth and sixth graders. She says it's not like Sunday school or church. It sounds like fun."

When Doris first asked me to go, I had refused but changed my mind when I heard her and Iris Skinner talking about Brother Ralph teaching them a Bible verse. I can't explain what came over me, but I felt compelled to look that snake in the grass right in the eye. I was sure God would give me a plan to get rid of him.

"Please, Mama?"

"When do they meet?"

"Every Wednesday at three o'clock in the church basement."

"Who's the teacher?"

"Mrs. Terry."

Mama sighed and searched my face trying to guess what was going on in my head. She didn't like the idea, however, Mama did Mrs. Terry's linens, and I knew they were friendly.

"All right, but you stay with Doris while you're in that building. The entire time, you hear me? And come straight home afterward." She shook her head and bent down to pull more weeds. I pulled weeds like it was the most important thing in the world.

The next Wednesday, I went to Sunshine Club. We played a word game and looked up the answers in the Bible. During music time, Mrs. Terry played hymns by Bach and told us how he made his living playing the organ in churches. I was having such a good time, I forgot about Brother Ralph until he came to teach the Bible verse.

"Hi, boys and girls," he boomed, quickly printing the verse in large letters on the blackboard. He smiled and looked at our upturned faces. "Let's say it together: 'Be ye kind, one to another.'"

He didn't see me at first. Sometimes you don't see what you don't expect. When he recognized me, his eyes widened, and his smooth cheeks reddened. I stared up at him trying to look inscrutable, a word I learned recently. When I put my hand up and asked him how to be kind to bad people, he turned to Mrs. Terry, whispered something and bounded up the stairs. I thought Mrs. Terry was a little put out with him, but she tried not to show it.

The next week, Brother Ralph was looking for me. There I was, inscrutable as ever. He wrote a line from The Lord's Prayer. "Forgive us our trespasses as we forgive those who trespass against us." As we recited together, he avoided looking at me and wiped perspiration from his forehead with a big white handkerchief. I didn't ask any questions, but he left in a hurry. I was pleased that my being there seemed to bother him, but I wondered why he didn't leave Duddley. I knew better than to tell Mama about it, so I spent a lot of time talking to God.

The next Wednesday, Doris and I walked to Sunshine Club together.

"Doris," I said, "have you noticed something different about Brother Ralph?"

"What do you mean?"

"I don't see it all the time, but every once in a while, especially when he's giving us the Bible verse, I think I see a faint glow above his head."

Doris is as levelheaded as they come, but she went for it hook, line and sinker.

"Oh, Roscoe Ann, I wouldn't be surprised. My mama says Brother Ralph's a saint. He really knows his Bible and he's so kind and thoughtful."

"Well, today," I said, "be sure and watch, especially when he looks at us and explains the verse. I can't be sure, but I know you have a good eye."

"I'll watch every move he makes. Thanks for telling me."

Brother Ralph picked up on Doris right away. She didn't realize she looked inscrutable. In the middle of reciting the verse, he began coughing and choking, finally running up the stairs like something was after him. Mrs. Terry said we should pray for Brother Ralph.

"I didn't see anything," Doris said as we walked away from the church, "but I think that's because he got that coughing fit."

"Didn't see what?" Iris Skinner came up behind us.

I looked at Doris, raised my eyebrows and shrugged my shoulders. Doris jumped right in.

"Roscoe Ann sees a glow over Brother Ralph's head."

"You mean a halo?" Iris caught her breath.

I couldn't believe it was so easy.

"It's not all the time. Just when he's giving us the Bible verse," Doris said, like she'd seen it too.

"Do you think we should tell some of the other kids?" Iris asked.

Oh, happy day, I thought. As we walked, Doris and Iris planned who to tell—definitely not parents.

"They'll laugh at us," Iris said.

"Or say we're blaspheming," said Doris.

I hoped this wasn't getting out of hand but didn't say anything.

The next Wednesday when Brother Ralph stood before us, I looked around and was amazed at the faces peering up at him. No one realized they looked inscrutable. Brother Ralph looked miserable. He stumbled through the verse and skipped telling us to memorize it. Without a word to Mrs. Terry, he rushed up the stairs, wiping perspiration from his face. Mrs. Terry shook her head.

Doris and Iris were disappointed. The other kids thought we were nuts.

Two days later, I stopped to see Grandma Dickey on my way home from the library.

Instead of asking me what I'd been up to, she said, "Have you heard about Brother Ralph?"

"No, ma'am." My heart skipped a beat.

"He's leaving," Grandma said. "Seems his health is failing." She shook her head. "Such a shame."

"That's too bad." I crossed my fingers behind my back. "What's the matter with him?"

"Seems Brother Ralph just gave out," Grandma said. "He couldn't sleep or eat and was jumpy as a cat on a hot tin roof. Mrs. Hinson told me this morning. Her husband's a deacon, you know? I thought Brother Ralph wasn't preaching as good these last few Sundays but figured it was just a slump. Everybody gets those."

"What do you suppose caused it?" I hoped he hadn't mentioned us kids.

"Oh ... uh." Grandma's cheeks turned pink. "Bad nerves."

"What are they going to do for a preacher?" I had trouble not jumping for joy.

"Mrs. Hinson says the deacons will be looking for a new preacher right away. A married man with a family this time."

"Why's that?"

"Oh ... uh." Grandma turned pink again. "Better nerves."

Mama was ironing when I got home. I sat at the table with my usual glass of milk and cookies.

"How was school?"

"Good." I wondered how to break the news. "I stopped to see Grandma."

"What's the latest in Duddley?"

"Brother Ralph's leaving town," I said matter-of-factly.

Mama didn't say anything for a moment, and I felt one of those "What aren't you telling me?" looks. Finally, she spoke.

"Did Grandma say why he decided to leave?"

"Mrs. Hinson told her it was failing health due to bad nerves."

Twenty-Fifth High School Reunion

"Please, Dan, I can't go by myself. If I don't show up with a husband, it won't matter what I say. I never dated in high school."

"Clarissa, if all you want to do is show up with a husband, then I'm sure as hell not going." The tall man seemed to unfold as he got up from the breakfast table, kissed the top of her head and loped out of the kitchen.

"Dan, please." Clarissa pulled the pink housecoat around her still slender body and plopped down at the kitchen table. Random gray strands highlighted the brown hair wrapped around her head in soft waves. There were more laugh lines than wrinkles in the almost smooth face and only slight signs of a second chin. She didn't realize that the years had treated her well. In her mirror, she saw gray hair, wrinkles, a double chin, a fuller bosom, the mother of four children who were nearly adults.

Several hundred miles away, in a different time zone, Nancy was sweating as she turned up the speed on her treadmill.

"Ms. Martin, you know you aren't supposed to readjust the rate. That's my job." The muscled young man with wild red curls shook his fingers at her. "This is your first day, and we gotta take it slow. One day at a time. Remember now." When he turned his back, she stuck her tongue out at him.

I only have six weeks. Why don't they plan these things earlier? I have got to lose at least thirty pounds. My God. That's five pounds a week! I'll never make it. I wish I could get Jody to do this. He's fat but being so tall he doesn't look as fat as I do.

"Fat and happy, Loveboat," he said. He opened another beer and changed the channel to football news.

"Well, I'm not happy. And don't call me Boat. I don't need reminding."

"Okay, let's us just stay home. I like being at home with you better anyway."

"They'd think we didn't come because we look such a mess."

"Now come on, Nancy. We don't look a mess. We look like a lot of other people our age who've done well in this world and live the good life. Nothing wrong with that. All those skinny ones probably go without good food to pay the rent on houses they can't afford."

"Well, I have six weeks, and I'm going to be skinnier even though you can afford to pay the rent."

Six weeks later a crowd of forty-somethings entered the gymnasium of Croft Falls High School.

"Dan, you look so handsome in your new suit." Clarissa adjusted his tie.

"It cost too much just to impress a bunch of people I'll never see again."

"They'll remember you and wonder how homely Clarissa Jenkins ever did it. I hope Nancy Clark is here. She was the class beauty.

Jody Martin was the football star. I hear they are still married. And rich."

"Was he quarterback for Tampa Tarpons?"

"I don't know the names of those teams, but it was one of the big ones. I always admired Nancy, but we weren't close friends."

After an hour of no host bar, they looked for their places at one of the round banquet tables. Seating was alphabetical, so the two couples met as they approached the table.

"Clarissa!"

"Nancy! Jody!"

The three classmates hugged, exclaiming how good they all looked. Finally, Dan cleared his throat.

"Oh, excuse me. This is my husband, Dan Mason. We celebrated our twentieth anniversary last month."

"We did number twenty-four last June," said Jody. He clapped a large arm around Nancy.

Two more couples joined them, and the conversation was as though the years had never been. Dan and the other non alum spouses found themselves included in the exchanges and laughter.

After dinner and a brief program, one of the organizers spoke.

"Don't forget, people. Be here tomorrow at 9 AM sharp for the ride out to Miller's Park. We're busing so that we have a designated driver. Dress comfortably. It'll be fun and games. All day. Now, the Croft Falls Six will play for your dancing pleasure."

"Aren't you glad you came, Dan?"

"Yes, Clarie, I am. You must have had a wonderful time growing up with all these warm, caring people."

"We weren't always as caring as we could have been. But yes, it was a good place to be."

Dan kissed her lightly on the lips and they danced with their arms around each other.

"Jody, this has been so good. What was I worried about? Clarissa is the only one of us who almost looks like she did twenty-five years ago. But I don't think she knows it. She never dated, did she?"

"I tried a time or two, but her old man wouldn't let her out of the house."

"Jody!"

"Come on, Loveboat, that was before I discovered you. She sure seems to have found herself a nice guy." Jody gave Nancy a big smooch, smearing her lipstick. She put her arms around his neck, and he pulled her close as they danced to the familiar music.

"I think I feel some bones," Jody said.

Only a Little Bit

"Does it hurt to be old, Gramma?" The little girl snuggled closer to the older woman and looked up at her wrinkled face. "Mama says getting old is just one ache after another."

"Well, she's right about the aches. But they sort of come and go." Gramma hugged Sara and kissed the top of her head.

"Well, I don't know if I want to be old." Sara loved the warm softness of her Gramma's body. "I don't like to feel bad."

"Getting old isn't just about aches and pains," Gramma said. "There are many things that take your mind off of it."

"What kinds of things?"

"As I get older, I don't seem to worry so much about things I can't change."

"Like what, Gramma?"

"Getting old for one thing." Gramma chuckled. "You can't change it, so you look for ways to live with it."

"You mean like coming to live with us even though you wanted to stay out on the farm after Grampa died?"

"Yes. That was a big one for me. But now that I've been here a while, it feels good. You all are fun to be with and you know what? I don't feel as old as I did out on the farm." Gramma smiled and patted Sara's cheek.

"Why's that?"

"For one thing, even though your mom's not my born daughter, she calls me 'Mother.' I like that. She's kind and very smart."

"That's cause she went to college," Sara piped.

"That's always a good thing to do, but your mom has an understanding heart. She saw I needed to be needed. Now I have my place like the rest of the family. Your mom asks me to help in the kitchen because she knows I like to cook. I try not to get in her way. We have some good conversations out in the garden too." Gramma paused. "When your daddy takes me to the doctor or dentist, he makes sure I have my list of medicines and am on time. Sometimes when we're driving, he asks about when he was growing up. He could be a rascal." Gramma laughed. "He's always cheerful about taking me places, though I know it isn't always convenient."

"Why's that?"

"Editing a newspaper, even a small one, is a big job, and though he puts in lots of hours, he never neglects us, his family. I'm real proud of your daddy."

"Me too." Sara snuggled again.

"One good thing about being old is nobody expects me to remember everything. I seem to recall what happened years ago, but yesterday can be a problem." Gramma chuckled.

"Oh, Gramma. You remember just fine. Besides I can help you with yesterday. It's the years when you were young that I like hearing about anyway. 'Specially about how you and Grampa fell in love and worked on the farm. Your story about how the goats got in the kitchen is one of my favorites." The little girl giggled.

"Yes, Sara. I have time to remember many events in my life. I didn't always understand why some things happened. I carried hurt and sometimes guilt. Now, looking back puts a different light on matters. I am able to let go of the hurt and guilt. I am a happier person." Gramma hugged Sara.

"I hope I can be like you when I'm old, Gramma. I'm glad it doesn't hurt."

"Only a little bit, Sara."

A Fine Cigar

"I have to get back to my room before seven," Grace said, getting up from the table where she always sat for Sunday dinner with her friends. "Jaimie usually calls at that time." She said the same thing every Sunday evening. Goodbyes were murmured as always. Diners watched the tall, straight, gray-haired woman make her way through the dining room and into the hall.

Grace glanced around and quickly moved to the stairway. She shunned the elevator in order to get some exercise and to prove she could still climb four flights of stairs. Grace was eighty years old. She had never encountered anyone on the stairs. Management discouraged use because of potential falls and injuries.

Tonight, upon entering the stairwell, she heard footsteps. When she stopped to listen, she heard a door open. There was a pause. Then it closed. Upon reaching the second landing, she smelled something familiar. Something she hadn't smelled in a long time. A fine cigar. She began to hurry, trying to catch the aroma and breathe it in.

"James? Can it be you?" She knew it wasn't, but she hurried up the next two flights anyway. The aroma lingered on the fourth and last landing. When she opened the door to her floor, she glanced down the hallway, hoping to see the cigar smoker. Grace surmised that he'd hurried to his room since smoking was forbidden in the building. She detected a faint cigar aroma in the hallway.

Grace entered her apartment still wondering who the smoker might be. Four men lived on the hallway, but she'd never seen them smoking. "It's someone like you, James." Grace had loved the smell of her husband's cigars. They were expensive, and he didn't smoke them frequently, but when he felt there was an occasion, he'd splurge. The first time was when he was promoted to first lieutenant six months before he expected it. James wasn't a cigarette smoker, but he loved good cigars. When Jaimie was born, he splurged. Cigars were offered to all the cadre in his company as well as the battalion commander and his staff.

Through the years, Grace saved from her household money and gave James his favorite cigars on his birthday. He made them last as long as possible.

Early on, Grace had asked to take a puff. Coughing and wiping tears from her eyes, she said, "My grief, James, how can you?" It surprised her that something smelling so good nearly made her throw up.

Sitting in her lounge chair, Grace realized this was the first time she'd smelled a good cigar since James died, eight years before. She closed her eyes and began to doze. Grace and James were dancing. He swept her around the floor, handsome in his dress blues with the new silver leaves on his epaulets. Grace wore the pink, full-length gown he loved. Gray flecked their hair, but their eyes sparkled with "I love you" at every glance. The orchestra played "Star Dust," their favorite song. The next week he would leave for Vietnam, but they pushed that thought away.

James came home after a year of war, unscathed, but different in little ways. Grace bought some cigars for a coming home present.

Their first evening alone, when they were having a drink before dinner, she brought them out. She clipped off the end, handed it to him and flicked the lighter.

"I never had one of these in Vietnam. There was nothing to celebrate." Finally, he placed the cigar between his lips. For a while, they sipped their drinks and inhaled the smoke. More of the old James returned after that.

Grace roused, still wondering who the cigar smoker might be. She didn't know any of the men well enough to ask if they'd been smoking where they weren't supposed to. Best to leave smoking dogs lie.

Several months later, Grace was leaving her apartment when the door to the stairwell opened. Eunice, a neighbor, looked out into the hallway for a moment and then came toward Grace.

"Hello, Grace," she said, hurrying to her apartment and keeping her hands in her pockets.

"Good evening," Grace said, inhaling the unmistakable cigar aroma. Walking quickly to the stairway, not daring to look back. she called, "You smoke a fine cigar, Eunice."

Whither Thou Goest

"Yes, Joanna, I always knew that John wasn't mine, but I'm glad you've finally told me." He reached over and patted the thin, age-spotted hand. "Funny though how much he was like me. Even looked a little like me. More so than our Matthew."

Joanna dried the tears at the corners of her eyes with a lace-edged handkerchief.

"At first I was afraid to tell you. I worried that you might find out and leave me. But then, we had Matthew, so I let it slide to the back of my mind."

"After a while, I never thought about it either. We were a family and that's what mattered."

"You gave us an abundant life, Elton."

"That all changed when the boys were killed in Vietnam. Somehow it didn't seem important anymore." Elton clinched his jaw and kept back the tears as he had done so many times.

"You're a good man, Elton."

"You've always been the best wife a man could have." He continued to hold her hand.

They watched as sunset colored the front porch of their farm home of fifty-seven years.

"Elton, do you remember the day we first saw this place? So wild, abandoned. I thought it was hopeless. Why couldn't I see what you saw? I hated being out here with the two little boys when I was sure we could do better in town."

"Yes, I remember. I was afraid, but something wouldn't let me give in. The thought of living and working in town scared me more than trying to make something of this place. I'm sorry you had to work so hard, but without you, I never could have made it."

"I can't be honest and say I didn't mind the hard work, but I guess it was good for me." Joanna laughed softly.

"It wasn't that good for either one of us. It gave us strong minds and determination, but look at us. My heart is due to go any day. No more surgery. No transplant. You've been in that wheel chair six years and need me more each day. I don't know how you've endured the pain."

"You've taken too good care of me," she said smiling at him. "If you hadn't been such a good nurse, I'd have made it to the other side long ago."

They sat silent for a while.

"What time will the people from Golden Age Care Center be here tomorrow?" Elton asked.

"Miss Smith said we should be ready by nine o'clock."

They continued to watch the colors change as the sun neared the tops of the hills. A flock of geese flew against the sky, calling out to one another.

"Let's take a ride." Elton patted Joanna's hand.

He wheeled her chair down the ramp to the driveway, toward the open garage. He helped her into the passenger side and got in behind the wheel. The motor started easily and idled. Elton reached up, pressed a small cartridge sitting on the dashboard and the garage door closed. They clasped hands.

"I love you, Joanna."

"I love you, Elton."

Halloween Ball

"I'll be glad when we get this evening behind us," Dale said, finishing up the scrambled eggs and taking a big swallow of coffee.

"Oh, it'll be fun. Especially since you and Josh got your way about the costumes." Jan sipped tea and spread jelly on an English muffin.

"It's a good idea," said Dale. "You girls enjoy all the falderal of costumes, but for guys it's different. Besides, with all of us dressed as ghosts, you ladies won't have our competition for the costume prizes."

Jan didn't bother to answer. She was thinking about the witch costume she planned to wear to the Country Club's annual fundraiser. Every year the group gave money to the local children's hospital, ensuring that no child went without medical care. Every year they chose a different holiday and this year was Halloween. The men rebelled against costumes but offered instead to come as ghosts since that was quick and easy. Most had to buy white sheets, but no one complained. Their wives or girlfriends slit and stitched openings for the eyes, nose and mouth.

That evening, Jan waited impatiently for Dale to arrive. This was one more time their plans were put on hold because of his work delivering babies. She knew what she faced when they married, but it didn't get easier. She even suspected he created delays when he wasn't keen on the occasion. Like tonight.

The phone rang. "Honey, sorry I'm running late. Mrs. Wilkins went to the hospital just now, and I have to go over and check on her. She's early, and I'm worried about this one."

"Dale. If this is your way of getting out of going to the ball—"

"No. This is for real. I'll be there as soon as I can. Promise. Love you."

Jan drove to the club. She checked the tote bag containing Dale's sheet at the coat room. She asked the attendant to watch for him. Soon she was socializing and even dancing with a couple of ghosts. They wouldn't tell her who they were. She recognized Brian Holloway when he tried to grope her. She gave him a dirty look and walked off the floor. It dawned on her that maybe the male contingent planned this as a means to get away with stuff. Wait 'til you get here, Dale, she thought.

A sumptuous buffet allowed guests to help themselves. Small, round tables for four circled the large ballroom. The evening was mild. Jan picked out a few things and chose an unoccupied table on the terrace. She turned her head for a moment looking for Dale. When she turned back to sit down, she was startled to see a ghost standing at the table. He was the same size as Dale, but she thought his eyes looked a little different. Just tired, she thought. He gave her a brief hug and pulled out her chair.

When she asked about Mrs. Wilkins, he gave her a thumbs-up. It became apparent he had decided not to talk. Instead, he nodded his head, used his hands and whispered. Jan noticed that many ghosts took off their costumes to eat more easily. Jan's ghost stayed hidden,

83

whispering that his clothes were the ones he'd worn all day. "I'd embarrass you." He didn't get anything to eat, claiming he'd had a sandwich earlier. He didn't drink the wine a waiter served. Jan was relieved no one joined them. Aggravated with Dale, she deliberately spoke as little as possible, as did he.

In a while, a small combo began to play. When they moved onto the floor, she was amazed at how smoothly he danced. He kept his hands hidden in the sheet. She thought they felt unusually soft. Gloves? Why?

"Have you been taking lessons?" she asked. He shrugged, chuckled and wrapped her in his arms. Feelings that hadn't been there in a long time enveloped her. She surprised herself when she whispered, "I love you, Dale."

He whispered, "Not as much as I love you," and held her tighter. The festering resentment receded. She wondered if things might change tonight.

There were prizes for different costumes. The men received none.

"Serves you right," said the chairwoman. "But we raised $100,000." The gathering clapped and cheered.

The evening was declared ended, and couples started leaving. Jan walked toward her car. Her ghost headed the opposite way. As she unlocked her car, she was surprised to see Dale running toward her. He was rumpled and disheveled.

"Oh, honey. I am so sorry." He explained that Mrs. Wilkins had delivered. "The baby almost died." His voice broke, and he took a deep breath. "Mrs. Wilkins is still in ICU but should be okay," he said, quietly. Jan saw deep concern in her husband's tired eyes.

"But we just ..." She told Dale about the ball. They looked at one another in wonder.

"Do you have any idea who he was?" Dale asked.

"I thought it was you." They held each other for a long moment.

At home, over a glass of wine, they talked more about the mysterious ghost. Dale put his arms around Jan when she shivered.

"I'll talk to the others," said Dale. "Surely he left some clue."

They went up the stairs, arm in arm. At the landing, a large window looked out over Jan's beautiful garden. The moonlight shone brightly on trees, shrubs and a variety of flowers.

"Jan," Dale pointed.

What looked like a large white sheet, circled the yard and flew up toward the window. No face was visible on the round head, but two hidden arms wiggle-waggled in the same way pilots acknowledge others. Then, it was gone.

Flash the Northern Flicker

"My goodness, Flash. You're a mess." Flossie, his mate, began to pick small bits of grass, and who knows what else, from the Northern Flicker's ruffled feathers. "What happened to you?"

"I'm not sure." He shook himself vigorously. Using his right talon, the flicker scratched something from his beak.

"Tell me all about it," Flossie said, smoothing his feathers. She fondly rubbed her beak against his.

"Well, I was out looking for something to eat and didn't find much in the trees. I flew out to the clearing where I spotted swarms of bugs—all kinds. They saw me coming and took off. I thought I had 'em, but some flew off one way, some another. A bunch of tasty looking ones headed for the big thing that sits out in the middle of the clearing."

"You mean the thing where those critters hide? Where the hairy one makes such a fuss?

"Yeah. That's the one."

"You didn't go over there?" Flossie whispered.

"Not on purpose. I wanted to swoop into that swarm and get a good gullet full. Next thing I know that swarm is trying to get into a round thing that sticks out of the big thing."

"Where white and gray clouds float sometimes?" Flossie shivered. "You never know when stuff is going to come out of there."

"Anyway, I was right on those bugs when they slipped down that round thing. Before I knew it, I was slipping too. It was dark, and I flapped like crazy trying to get out." Flash paused. "Next thing I knew something below opened up and let in fresh air and light. I thought I was going free. But then the racket started. Like birds I've never heard before. Really screechy. When they poked a tree limb up the round thing and hit me on the leg, I thought I was a goner. I tried to scoot up, but I couldn't get out. I hung on to the side of the round thing for dear life."

"Oh, Flash. You poor bird." Flossie thought it was a miracle that he was beside her now. "What happened then?"

"The noise stopped, and I saw light under me and breathed fresh air. I found that by spreading my wings, I could slowly slide down the sides of the round thing. But suddenly it wasn't there. I fell into a heap of something soft and dusty. I could hardly breathe. One of those critters came at me with something that looked like a strip of bark, only it bent. He tried to catch me with it, but I scrambled away. I think he was afraid too. Even though I was out of the round thing, expecting to come home, I couldn't see sky or trees. I flew up and banged my head on something hard. Flossie, I was inside the critters' thing in the clearing, and I didn't know how to get out."

Flossie shook her head. Flash continued.

"I swooped low and fast, trying to scare them. They screeched and waved those bark strips as if they wanted to hit me. I flew as high as I could and saw an opening. I flew into it, but there was no way out. In the meantime, one of those critters came after me. He didn't fly but ran up on something. I thought he had me. I flew into another opening, but it didn't go anywhere either. Something funny about that place, Flossie. When I was up there and looking for the way out, I thought I saw birds when I flew from one opening to another. They looked like me and moved when I did. I wondered if the critters planned to keep me there if I were caught.

"How awful, Flash. Maybe we should move deeper into the woods."

"Well, I decided to look for the round thing again. I hoped I'd get out the same way I got in, but I couldn't find it. Both those critters ran around waving the bark, trying to catch me. I swooped at them, and they really screeched. I was getting dizzy flying around in that thing. I perched to rest, but whatever it was wobbled and scared me. Finally, on a particularly low swoop, I misjudged, and one of those critters caught me in a strip. Only it wasn't like bark."

"Oh, my goodness, Flash. What was it?" Flossie shivered.

"Something soft. Didn't hurt a bit. But I couldn't see anything and I knew those critters were taking me somewhere. Screeching like crazy. Suddenly they opened the soft strip and threw me up in the air. I was outside the thing and saw our woods. I flew so fast I almost hit the first tree I came to. I didn't stop until I got home." His wings drooped. "I'm worn to a frazzle."

"Oh, Flash. I'm so thankful you're safe." Flossie nuzzled his beak. "I found a lot of fresh berries while you were gone. Would you like some?"

Flash tucked his head beneath a wing and hunkered down. He was fast asleep. Flossie stroked his feathers.

The Piano

Elizabeth saw the ad in Sunday's paper: Beloved grand piano for sale. Must play to appreciate. There was no telephone number, only a street address in the old section of town. She knew it was mostly old brownstones that had been turned into apartments.

"I'm just going to look. It never hurts to look," she told Nicholas. "We need more furniture to fill this large room. Besides, I miss having a piano. I could take a few students to help with our bills."

"After your breakdown, you vowed you would never play again," Nicholas said, looking up from a book.

"I know, and I don't plan to ever concertize again. Dr. Klein said now that I am recovering, I should find an interest to fill my time. When I asked, he said going back to music might be difficult, but also healing."

Nicholas looked at Elizabeth for a moment, remembering that Dr. Klein had advised him not to create stress for his wife. "You'll know," he said, reaching for her hand and kissing it gently.

"I promise not to spend too much." She smiled, kissed the end of her index finger and tapped his nose. They both chuckled.

When Elizabeth arrived at the address, she was pleased to see that it was a private residence. The doorbell set off faraway chimes, and the heavy door soon opened. A very old man smiled at her. His clear blue eyes made Elizabeth think of someone much younger.

Tall, slender and slightly stooped, a cap of tightly curled gray hair covered his head.

"Madam?"

"I've come to see the piano you advertised," Elizabeth said. "If you still have it?"

"Oh, yes. It is here. Please come in." He spoke with a slight accent that Elizabeth recognized as German.

He opened the door wider, stepped to the side and motioned her in with a restrained bow. Elizabeth felt something irresistible drawing her, but it didn't frighten her. Looking about, she had expected something grander than the narrow, steep stairway to the second floor. The pendulum hung motionless in a black grandfather's clock. Dust covered everything. Elizabeth walked carefully onto the worn oriental carpet.

"I am Albert Grosmann," the old man announced as though she should recognize him. "May I take your wrap?" He hung it on a coat tree that stood near the table. Before Elizabeth could introduce herself, a querulous voice came from upstairs.

"Albert?" Elizabeth didn't understand the labored. raspy flow of words that followed, because it was German. Albert answered, then spoke to Elizabeth.

"It is Louisa, my sister. She wishes to know who is here. I said you have come to see our piano."

Though she spoke with difficulty, Louisa continued what sounded like a tirade. Albert stood patiently until the woman stopped. Gently, caringly, he replied. She made no answer.

"My sister, she is quite ill and confined to her bed. I must sell to pay for her medications." He sighed. "The piano has been in our family for three generations. Louisa began playing when she was four years old. As a young woman, she toured Europe, North and South America. She has played for the Emperor in Japan. So many prizes, accolades. Then the illness came."

"I'm so sorry," Elizabeth said. Albert shrugged his shoulders.

"It was a good life," he continued. "I never performed, but for twenty years I presented her to the world. She was, as you would say, sensational." The memories carried him away for a moment. Elizabeth wracked her brain to recall a concert pianist named Louisa Grosmann. Perhaps she used a stage name?

"Come. It is in the parlor." He slid two dark paneled doors open and led her into a room where the November afternoon sun struggled through dingy lace curtains that covered tall windows. A few pieces of Victorian furniture seemed lost in the large room. One floor lamp and a small sewing rocker sat in a corner near a wall of half-empty bookshelves that reached from floor to ceiling. A tall glass cabinet held a few pieces of fine porcelain. Faded photos sat on the mantel over a closed fireplace. It was obvious. Albert had already sold some of the family treasures. Large faded squares and rectangles on the walls evidenced the removal of artwork.

Elizabeth was saddened by the ebbing colors in the Aubusson carpet that covered most of the dusty hardwood floor. She followed Albert to the far end of the room toward a blue velvet drapery that covered the entire wall. He reached for a cord and opened the center panels, revealing a recessed alcove covered in the same fabric. A crystal chandelier hung over a grand piano standing on a dais. The piano was burnished to a high luster. There wasn't a speck of dust on it. Elizabeth gasped at its majestic beauty. To the side, an easel held a portrait of a beautiful young woman sitting at this piano. She wore a white formal gown, her hair arranged in an early 1900s fashion. For several moments Elizabeth thought she heard a Chopin waltz until Albert's voice reminded her of his presence.

"The piano. It is beautiful, is it not?" At first, she wondered if he had also heard the waltz, but his expression revealed nothing.

"The piano is beautiful," she said, wondering who this man was.

"Would you like to play something?" It sounded more like a challenge than an invitation. Elizabeth hesitated, unable to refuse. A subtle force, much like the one when she entered the house, drew her. Her fingers touched the keys knowingly, effortlessly. She saw the notes in her head and heard the pure, perfect music. Her hands seemed gloved in warmth and dexterity. She caressed the keys as she played. She could not have struck a wrong note had she tried. Elizabeth came to the end of the piece and sat still for several moments. When she removed her hands, the warm, easy feelings disappeared. She quickly went through the mental exercise the therapist taught her when she felt anxiety returning.

Albert interrupted her thoughts. "You have unusual technique, Madam."

Elizabeth got up from the bench and smiled at Albert. "I will take the piano." Again, she heard a Chopin waltz.

Four Friends

"Police are looking for a serial killer. This morning a young woman's body was found in an alley behind Acme Storage and Shipping. No identification of this third victim has been made. The first homicide occurred in a deserted section of downtown. The second victim was found in Cramden Park. The killer picks a dark, lightly traveled place in the early morning hours. He breaks his victim's back, rapes her and strangles her with a cord. The search is being intensified. You are warned to stay out of dark, isolated parts of town. If you have information, please contact the police."

Martha turned off the television. Ethel, Susan and Marlene shook their gray heads.

"What are we going to do?" asked Martha.

These lifelong friends, in their mid-seventies except for Marlene who was sixty-eight, lived in a retirement center for teachers. None had married, dedicating their skills to children. They were extraordinarily hearty and agile, mentally and physically. Susan had a black belt in Karate. In their classrooms they had been able to set things right, to take action when behavior got out of hand. They talked at length about the murders and how it was affecting the entire town. "What can we do?"

Several mornings later, at one o'clock, they drove away from the retirement center, Ethel at the wheel of her Chevrolet Impala. Slender Marlene wore a short, tight-fitting black dress with a pink, fake fur jacket. Her legs were still good, and she was able to walk seductively in high heels. Skillful make-up and a long blonde wig completed her disguise. The others wore black sweatshirts and pants with black tennies. Face masks were pulled up on the black ski caps. Ethel brought a tote bag containing a thermos of coffee, paper cups and homemade cookies.

"Why the coffee and cookies?" Susan asked.

"You never know," Ethel said.

Nothing happened that first morning nor the rest of the week. Marlene walked in lonely places downtown, through the industrial area, through Cramden Park. Ethel drove close enough to keep her in sight. During the second week as they were cruising downtown, a police car came out of a side street and pulled up next to Marlene. Ethel quickly caught up, and they all jumped out.

"Oh, honey," Ethel shrilled. "We've been looking for you everywhere."

Marlene turned, scowled and screeched, "Go away! I won't go home. I'm going to a party." She swung her small beaded purse at Ethel who dodged.

"What's the trouble, ma'am?" asked the police officer.

"My sister doesn't always remember who she is, or where she is, but it'll be all right, officer. My friends will help me get her home." Martha and Susan smiled and nodded. Turning to Marlene, Ethel said, "I've brought some cookies, dear."

Marlene snatched a proffered cookie and stuffed it into her mouth.

"I have some coffee too." Ethel smiled at the officers. Soon everyone was having coffee and cookies. Marlene, sullen but no longer combative, suddenly yelled, "I wanna go home." The officers drove away, satisfied the situation was in capable hands.

It was getting late, but the women decided to swing through Cramden Park since it wasn't too far out of the way. Ethel drove slowly without lights, able to see by a bright moon.

"There he is!" they whispered in unison. Ethel pulled over near shrubs growing close to the road. Marlene got out of the car and walked quickly toward a tall, athletic figure strolling along the road ahead, unaware of the car. Marlene hurried. Ethel, Martha and Susan pulled the masks over their faces.

"Hi, handsome," Marlene said when she caught up.

The young man turned to look at her, unable to penetrate the disguise in the shadows.

"Hi, Blondie." He peered closely.

"Would you like some company?" Marlene pitched her voice invitingly. but a sudden cough caused her to turn away, revealing a wrinkled, corded throat.

In an instant, the man grabbed her by the neck, shaking her violently. He pulled a length of nylon cord from his jacket pocket.

"You, old hag. What do you think you're doing?" he snarled.

"My God. Whoever got this guy meant business. Doc says his back is broken in a couple of places like he was stomped on."

"That blow to his right temple must have put him out like a light."

"The cord around his neck makes you think of that serial killer's MO."

"Don't it though?"

"I wonder what all this pink stuff is. Looks like some kind of fur."

"Chief says there was quite a scuffle."

The two men placed the body on a gurney and wheeled it toward a waiting van.

"The police are investigating the death of a young man found early today in Cramden Park. Release of his name is pending notification of next of kin. We have learned from an unidentified source that the police are checking his DNA against samples from three young women who were recently murdered in our city. All died from strangulation with a nylon cord, much like one found near the victim. The police are looking for more than one attacker. Anyone who has information relating to this homicide is urged to call police."

Martha turned off the television. The four friends looked at one another complacently and raised their wine glasses.

House for Sale

"This house is a home. Built to last. Secure neighborhood. Priced right," was how Mary Sims, real estate salesperson, phrased the multiple listing. Mary was relieved when someone responded because sales were down, and she wasn't sure about this one.

The Winstons, first time home buyers, accompanied Mary up the front sidewalk.

"Oh, Jerry. Isn't this a sweet little house? The blue door and shutters are so welcoming. It just nestles into the yard, doesn't it?" Emily was smitten, oblivious of the shaggy shrubs and dandelion infested yard. Jerry looked at the weathered gray vinyl siding and broken ribs in the shutters.

They walked through the front door into a small foyer paneled in dark wood. A stairway climbed steeply up the right side of the narrow hallway. Mary guided them through a door to the left.

"This is the living room. The previous owner died recently and the heirs lost no time in emptying the house and putting it up for sale. It may need a few upgrades." Mary felt she'd fulfilled her professional duty.

"Oh, Sweetie," Emily chirped, "a stone fireplace." The entire hearth was blackened after many years of burning and little cleaning. It smelled. Jerry ran his hand across the heavy varnished plank that served as the mantel. It had collected dust for a long time.

"This fireplace makes the room," Emily said. "Imagine snuggling on our own couch, watching the fire sparkle and leap, a large holly wreath over the mantel. Oh, Dearest, I can see it now, can't you?"

She didn't wait for his answer as she followed Mary into a kitchen that was long and narrow, running the width of the house. The cabinets, nicked and scratched, were a dull green, popular many years ago. Stains in various shades of beige and brown colored an otherwise clean sink. The faucet dripped. The floor covering was more recent, obviously a do-it-yourself job, buckling at the sink. An old refrigerator and older gas range looked exhausted.

"This will require some updating," Emily said, "Can't you just see white cabinets with glass doors and a small table for two at the window?"

Jerry grunted as he peered through a narrow window framing an overgrown backyard.

"Of course," Emily continued, "it would be a good idea to enlarge the window for a better view of the yard. You could build some bird feeders, Honey."

Emily took his arm and steered him through a door at the far end of the kitchen and into the dining room. An outdated, corroded light fixture dangled from the ceiling. Along one wall was a built-in china cupboard, an obvious afterthought. Jerry judged it to be the work of the kitchen do-it-yourselfer. Heavy, square pieces of wood, coated with dark varnish promised a permanence that gave Emily pause but not for long.

"You could do something with that, couldn't you, Jerry?" Jerry bit his lip.

Upstairs, they looked at three bedrooms and two bathrooms. Emily saw girls in one of the bedrooms and boys in another, describing to Jerry the furnishings and color schemes she envisioned.

The slightly larger bedroom became a bower of marital bliss in Emily's plans. The adjoining musty bathroom needed a little work, though the hall bath needed a major renovation. "But you have to expect that in an older house, right Mary?

"Oh, yes," Mary chimed in, not having felt the need to say anything up to now. She was amazed at how the house seemed to be selling itself, at least to Emily.

As they went downstairs, Emily didn't seem to hear the creaks in the steps. Jerry caught a splinter in his thumb when he grasped the worn railing.

Emily started toward the living room, but Jerry took her arm.

"Em, we need to get along. Our other appointment is at three."

"You're right, Dear Heart. This sweet little house made me forget the time."

Mary started to suggest they go down to the basement where a gas furnace, in good working order, had been installed just two years ago. Before she could finish, Jerry grabbed Emily by the hand and practically ran down the sidewalk to their car.

"We'll be in touch," Emily called.

As they settled into the car, Emily said, "Don't you just love that little house?"

"No."

Emily turned and looked at Jerry in disbelief, "I thought you liked its charm and hominess."

"No."

"Don't you think we should consider it? It has all kinds of possibilities."

"No, Emily. That place is a dump. Rundown, smelly and dirty. The wiring and plumbing are outdated. It would take a pile of money to make it livable; a mint to make it the way you want it. It's overpriced."

Emily stuck out her lower lip. Jerry stuck out his chin, gunned the car and sped away. Blocks later, Emily sighed and read aloud the ad for the next house they were going to look at.

"Georgian, brick. Old world charm. Quiet neighborhood. Priced right."

The Black Hole

Helen stood at the graveside while the others moved away, giving the young widow a chance to say her last goodbye. Her mother and older brother, Fred, hoped she would be able to cry. Three cemetery workers remained out of sight in deference to Mrs. Robert Criston whose husband lay in the casket about to be interred.

Helen's inner voice spoke: Why did you come in along the ship channel? The fog was like soup. You had no business taking that shortcut. Bobby, I hate you, hate you. No, I don't. I will always love you, but this makes me so damn mad. I feel like spitting on your coffin. That would start some talk, wouldn't it? You'd probably get a laugh out of it. What am I going to do without you? Oh, Bobbie, I love you so.

Helen put her fingers to her lips and bent to touch the casket. Her legs gave way, and she fell onto the blanket of flowers covering her husband. Her brother reached her first and heard the deep, wrenching sobs. Her body heaved and shook. He heard her whispering, "Bobbie, Bobbie, please don't leave me."

"She's finally grieving and that's good," Dr. Steiner told the family. "Crying is part of healing. She's young and will recover."

Helen wept, sobbed and moaned for a week. Dr. Steiner gave her something that made her sleep, but when she awoke, the reality rushed in and swept her away into tears again. Her mother and brother began to worry because she ate so little. Again, the doctor assured them.

Finally, the crying stopped, but Helen insisted on staying in her childhood bedroom at the family home. She spent most of her time in bed, asleep and awake. She went to the table to eat but always returned to her room.

Fred brought in a small television. Though it was on most of the time, Helen lay with her eyes closed or with her back to it. Her mother had to remind her to shower and brush her teeth. Helen refused to see any of her friends. Fred, his wife Janet, and Helen's mother spent many hours sitting in the bedroom to be there if she stirred. This continued for three months, Dr. Steiner suggested grief counseling or a support group.

"Leave me alone," Helen said each time.

One day Fred suggested that he take her over to her house while he did some chores. "You can check up on things and tell me if there's something I've forgotten to look after." He hoped she would begin to take interest in the flowers she had nurtured.

"I can't go back there. Everything will remind me of Bobbie. I'm trying to forget him," she snapped.

"Hibernating in your mother's house doesn't seem to be helping," he said.

Helen heard the exasperation in his voice. She sat up and put her legs over the side of the bed. She shook her finger at him. "Hibernating!" she shrilled., "what do you know about having your heart ripped out? You and Janet go along like nothing has happened. Oh, I guess it scares you when you realize that it could have been you. But you don't know anything about losing the only one you've ever loved. You don't begin to know the loneliness. It's a big black hole that doesn't go away. Hibernating? I'm here because I don't know how to die."

She jumped to the floor and ran into the bathroom, slamming the door.

"You're not going to die as long as you're so busy feeling sorry for yourself," Fred yelled at the closed door and then wished he hadn't.

When she was sure Fred was gone, Helen came out of the bathroom, walked over to the closet and opened it. She saw a pair of blue jeans, a red polo shirt and a pair of leather sandals she always wore. She didn't know that Fred and her mother had brought over some of her things, praying for the day she'd be Helen again. She realized suddenly how much they loved her, remembered their patience and caring. Tears came, but she quickly wiped them away. Her inner voice spoke: You're right, Fred. I haven't been facing up to anything. I've been hibernating, feeling sorry for myself. What do I do now?

"Put on your clothes and use some lipstick." It wasn't audible, but she heard it in her heart. "Bobbie, is that you? she whispered." There was no answer, but Helen's entire being lightened as she shed her robe and pulled on her favorite pair of jeans. She felt a coolness on her right cheek, almost a kiss, as she went down the stairs.

Margot's Visitor

Margot roused and listened but kept her eyes closed. The television blared so she felt rather than heard someone moving about the room. It's not Julius, she thought, he's a smart cat but he can't open doors. The television screen no longer flashed against her eyelids. Someone was standing between her and the set. Her eyes flew open when a sharp blow to the footrest caused the chair to bounce into upright position.

"Wake up old lady." The voice was low and whispery.

Margot's sight was limited without glasses and recent sleep fogged her vision even more. Finally, she made out a figure of medium height. She blinked several times and saw long, shaggy, shoulder-length hair. A dark knit watch cap covered the forehead. A pulled-up turtleneck obscured the chin, Well-worn overalls and a baggy, soiled, tweed blazer hung on whatever it was. Shapeless athletic shoes had no strings and gaped around bare ankles. The whole thing reeked.

"What kind of varmint are you?" Margot asked, reaching for her glasses.

"Watch your mouth, old lady. I don't aim to hurt you so don't make me mad." The voice quavered slightly.

Margot peered more closely. This is a scared child, trying to scare me. And doing a good job.

"Just what do you want?" Margot asked.

"I want your money. I been all over this house. Where do you keep it?"

"I don't keep it anywhere because I don't have any this time of the month."

"What do you mean?" The voice rose a bit with disbelief.

"My money is Social Security, and it comes the first of the month. This is the 20th. I done spent it all. Now you get out of here. You're smelling up my house. You stay much longer, and I'll need a fumigator, and I sure can't afford that."

Just then a muscle in Margot's right hip contracted in pain, causing her to yelp and stand up. The figure moved backward, pulled a handgun out of the blazer pocket and pointed it at Margot who thought she saw a tremor in the hand.

"Oh, Lordy." Margot gasped in pain as much as fear. Standing caused the pain to subside.

"I don't want to shoot you. I'm hungry. That's why I need money. You got any food?" The voice was insistent.

"Yeah, I do. Tell you what. You step outside on the back porch, and I'll fix you a plate of eggs and grits, bacon and a big glass of milk." Margot paused.

"You think I'm some kind of looney? I step outside that door, you'll lock me out and call the sheriff." The intruder kept the gun pointed at her. Margot tried not to let it rattle her.

"First of all," Margot said, "the door lock is broken. That's how come you got in. You can watch through the screen, and if I move to the phone which is across the room from the stove, well. you'll have plenty of time to shoot me."

"Okay, but you better not try anything."

The trespasser slipped out the back door and stood in the shadows while Margot fixed a meal quickly and generously; four eggs, four slices of bacon, extra butter on the grits and lots of blackberry jelly on four slices of toast. She filled a large glass with milk. Her guest opened the screen door, and Margot set the plate and glass on a well-worn picnic table.

"Thank you, ma'am," The voice was almost a whisper.

The courtesy surprised Margot. "You're very welcome, I'm sure." She couldn't see the gun.

Margot's guest rummaged in a coat pocket, and Margot was amazed when a large workman's bandana appeared and was smoothed across the diner's lap. From the same pocket came a bottle of hand sanitizer. The clean hands were smooth and unblemished. Long slender fingers picked up the knife and fork and used them precisely. Margot was puzzled as she watched; no wolfing down, no slurping or dribbling as the food disappeared.

"May I please have some more milk?"

Margot went to the refrigerator and glanced toward the phone across the room.

"Don't think about it." The disheveled figure stood just outside the screen door, pointing the gun.

"I was thinking you might like some cookies I got in the cabinet over there," Margot said.

"Okay."

Margot took the tin of cookies out to the table.

"I don't see how you eat so good, but don't have no money?"

"Well, I won't eat so good now."

Margot watched, remembering a boy, Jason, from another time. He, too, had called her Old Lady instead of Mother. I wonder if anyone ever fed him when he was hungry. Did he ever smell that bad? The memories weighed in, and she spoke before considering what she was saying.

"If you put that gun away, I've got a proposition for you."

"What do you mean?" Suspicion was strong.

"You said you were looking for money to buy food. You haven't eaten in a good while, have you?" For the first time, Margot saw her guest's eyes. They were the same deep blue as Jason's but fringed with longer lashes, almost feminine.

"No, ma'am." Underneath the dirt, the features were fine and unmarked by stubble. The stance could have belonged to any young person. Margot looked closely at her visitor.

"I got some chores around here that need doing. Like I told you, I don't have money. You could stay around for a couple of days and help me get things cleaned up. I'll feed you. Give you a dry place to sleep." She glanced at a shed that stood away from the house.

"Yes, ma'am. I can do that." Margot thought she saw relief in the young face.

"A couple of other things," Margot said. "You have to give me the bullets to your gun."

"Why do you want the bullets?"

"If you got a gun with no bullets, and I got bullets with no gun, nobody's going to get shot."

"Yeah, but what's going to keep you from calling the sheriff? I broke into your house. I pulled a gun on you." The young person's voice shook.

"You got to trust somebody sometime. I think maybe this is your time. You got to trust that I need work done more than I care about calling the sheriff. I got to trust that you aren't going to hit me on the head with that gun when I'm not looking."

The young woman stared at the old woman. To Margot's surprise, she handed her the gun. It was lighter than she expected. A child's toy.

"There are no bullets," the girl whispered.

Mousey Brown

Mousey Brown and Rodentia Luv were mouse sisters. They lived in a very old house. The elderly woman who lived alone in the house had a tender heart.

The little mice liked to dine in the open garbage container under the kitchen sink. They were careful not to leave a mess, so the old woman didn't mind their coming and going.

One day, things changed.

"Oh Gran, he's such a sweet kitten, and he always uses his sandbox," said a young, treble voice. "He'll be good at mousing."

"I don't need a mousing cat."

"He needs a home. Please, Gran."

Mousey and Rodentia peeked between the curtains that hung in front of the sink. They saw a white, furry kitten with gray markings above his eyes, gray boots on his feet and a bushy tail.

Terrified, the little sisters ran back to their nest in the dining room wall.

"That's the creature Mother warned us about," said Mousey. "He's a cute kitten now, but someday he'll be a big cat." Mousey shivered.

"What will we do?" asked Rodentia.

"I have to think," snapped Mousey.

They didn't get much sleep that night, clinging together and shivering at the least sound.

The next day, when they got hungry, they crept through the hole in the wall under the sink. They peeked between the curtains. No kitten was in the basket nearby. The only sounds were the clock ticking and the refrigerator humming.

"Maybe he's gone."

"You're a dreamer, Rodentia. We'd better hurry."

They found a couple of tasty morsels and SWISH, the kitten's head came through the curtains. The sisters ran for the hole, but a furry paw caught Rodentia's tail and held it to the floor. Mousey watched in horror, then SQUEEEEEEKED! as loud as she could.

The startled kitten fell backward and the sisters escaped. They shivered for a long time in their nest behind the dining room wall.

"What are we going to do?" asked Rodentia.

"I don't know," said Mousey. "Just let me think."

The next morning, the sisters took different passages to the kitchen. Rodentia went the usual way to the hole behind the sink. Mousey went to the hole across the room behind the refrigerator. She crept along the narrow space between the refrigerator and a cabinet wall. She saw the kitten lying in his basket near the sink, eyes closed.

Mousey stood at the front of the refrigerator waiting until Rodentia peeked between the curtains and gave her the high sign that meant she was ready to take food out of the garbage container and put it in the passage.

Mousey planned to get the kitten's attention, and then run for safety in the space between the refrigerator and cabinet when he came for her. He was too big to follow. She would tease him until Rodentia gave the "finished" signal.

Rodentia waved the "ready" sign, and Mousey stepped out giving her best SQUEEEEK!

The kitten looked around but didn't move from his basket.

"What was that?" he asked, looking at Mousey.

After a pause, Mousey said, "It's Mouse Speak." She tried not to let her voice quiver.

"Mouse Speak? Hmm. Is 'mousing' Mouse Speak?"

He remained in his basket and yawned. Mousey had an idea.

"Yes, and it's very important," she said. "We mice are so small that we often need help. Mousing is helping a mouse in need. How nice of you to ask." She smiled broadly. The kitten smiled too.

"Hey, I like that. The way my person talked, I began to think it might be scary. By the way, my name's Kendall. What's yours?"

After introductions, the three had brunch under the sink.

"We mustn't leave a mess," Mousey said as she brushed food bits from Kendall's whiskers.

"This stuff is good," said Kendall, "much better than those things in my dish. Yeck!"

"We like this," Mousey paused, not wanting to mention poison or traps, "because it's good for us."

"It seems like you're helping me, instead of me helping you. What is Mouse Speak for that?" The kitten purred.

"That, Kendall, is 'befriending,'" said Mousey. "We want to be your friends."

Rodentia nodded her head. Kendall purred his loudest. Mousey sighed contentedly.

Snook and Maddie

"Get a grip on yourself, Maddie. This shouldn't take too long and the fresh air will do you good." Snook and his friend were on their way to work for Mrs. Peabody. Earlier, Snook had gone out to the older woman's place, picked up her car, brought it in for gasoline and oil change. He did a couple of errands for her. When he saw Maddie, he knew it would be a long day.

"Easy for you to say," Maddie croaked. "You didn't drink any of that shine last night. Arrgh."

Maddie's face turned green. Snook thought he'd have to stop the car right in the middle of the town square. If Maddie let go, they'd both be in a fix. The square was already busy, and the old fogies were on their favorite benches, soaking up spring sunshine. Nothing missed their bleary, squinty eyes. A good barf at 10 AM, in the town's pride and joy, would cause no end of trouble. Barf in Mrs. Peabody's Packard sedan would be even worse.

"Can you hold it?" Snook glanced at the bent over figure.

"Yeah, if you go a little faster."

Snook picked up speed as they left the square and headed out to the country. Maddie held his head in his hands and didn't turn green again. Soon the well-preserved Packard was purring up a drive lined with large pin oaks. They drove around to the rear of a well-kept antebellum house surrounded by flowers and a lawn in need of its weekly mowing.

"Maddie, you go on out to the shed and get the mower. I'll talk to Miz Peabody and see what she wants done inside. Don't you dare barf 'til you get behind the shed. You hear?"

"Yeah, yeah." Maddie was turning green again.

Snook picked up two books and two large grocery sacks from the back seat, slamming the door so Mrs. Peabody couldn't say he'd snuck up on her.

"That you, Snook?" came a sharp, querulous voice.

"Yes, ma'am."

A small, white-haired, frowning woman stood inside the screened door, opening it for Snook.

"Where's Maddie?"

"He's gettin' started on the yard."

"It's about time you got here. I was beginning to think ya'll were lost," the older woman said. "I got some extra things for you to do today, you hear?"

"Yes, ma'am." Snook hurried through the screened porch into a large kitchen. He placed the bags on the table and handed Mrs. Peabody the library books.

"I hope they gave you the right ones. Did you remember to get the lemon oil furniture polish? I want you to do the dining room today."

Snook winced inwardly. That would be a long job with those big pieces of furniture and the intricate carving. Hope Maddie can hold on, he thought.

"You'll have to clean the parlor carpet too. Those grandchildren! Here for three days and there are berry stains on the Aubusson. I told them not to eat in there. Then I found ink marks on the back of the downstairs bathroom door. It says something, but I couldn't make it out. Some kind of new dirty words probably."

"Yes, ma'am."

"Maybe Maddie can come in and help?"

"Oh, I don't know about that," Snook said, trying hard to think of how to keep Maddie out of the house. His heart hammered. Then he said, "We noticed weeds taking over the front beds, and the hedge needs cutting back too." He held his breath.

"Well, you know best about that, Snook. Ya'll work it out."

Mrs. Peabody began putting away the groceries, and Snook picked up the furniture polish. Several wrenching barfs came from outside, but Mrs. Peabody was placing things in the refrigerator and the motor labored loudly.

Snook sighed deeply when he realized what a long day it was going to be. He relaxed a bit when he heard the lawn mower start and begin moving. Mrs. Peabody went into the den where she turned on the television to watch her soap opera.

Snook was polishing the large dining table when he heard the lawn mower stop. He knew Maddie couldn't have finished already. Mrs. Peabody hadn't noticed. He decided he'd better check and quietly slipped out the front door.

He found Maddie lying unconscious beside the silent mower. He smelled of barf, and Snook saw remains on the front of his friend's shirt. Then he noticed a bleeding mark on Maddie's bare ankle. Cottonmouth Moccasins were common, especially around the creek that ran through Mrs. Peabody's place.

"Oh, Maddie. What do I do now?"

Maddie groaned.

"What's going on out there?" Mrs. Peabody called from the veranda.

"I think Maddie's been snake bit." Snook bent over his friend and checked to see if he was breathing. When he looked up, he was surprised to see Mrs. Peabody coming across the lawn. She used a walking stick but was beside the two young men in no time.

She knelt beside Maddie. "Where's the bite?" Snook bared Maddie's ankle.

"I think it might be a Cottonmouth," Snook said.

"Of course, it is," Mrs. Peabody snapped. "Run up to the house and call Dr. Dawson. You tell him I said it's Cottonmouth, and he needs to hurry. Then get me some clean towels out of the hall closet upstairs, and a basin of water." Snook took off running, and Mrs.

Peabody pulled Maddie onto her lap and made sure his leg and ankle were lower than his heart. "It'll be okay, Maddie." She noticed his soiled shirt. "I never saw a snake bite cause vomiting before."

When Snook came back, he held his friend while Mrs. Peabody carefully washed the fang mark on the boy's ankle. Maddie roused from his unconscious state.

"What happened?" He mumbled and coughed up a few pieces of barf.

Mrs. Peabody explained.

"Snakebite?" Maddie squealed.

Snook had to hold him tight. Mrs. Peabody put a wet cloth to Maddie's throat and continued to bathe the ankle.

"Don't need any more of that," she said.

Dr. Dawson drove up and came running. He'd made good time.

"It's just one strike," he said, "but that's enough for anybody." He took a vial and hypodermic needle from his black case and handed it to Mrs. Peabody. Snook didn't look to see what the doctor did with a small scalpel. When Dr. Dawson turned toward Mrs. Peabody, she handed him the loaded syringe. Maddie flinched when the needle pierced his skin.

"Let's get him to my car," said Dr. Dawson.

After Maddie was settled in the passenger seat, Mrs. Peabody checked to see if he was okay. "Remember, Maddie, you sit up straight. Use this if you feel sick again." She handed him the empty basin.

Snook and Mrs. Peabody walked back to the house. She took Snook's arm.

"You saved Maddie's life, Miz Peabody. I didn't know what to do."

"Thank you, Snook. It's been some years, but at one time I was a nurse."

"Well, you haven't forgotten anything. I could tell Dr. Dawson depended on you."

At the foot of the steps to the front veranda, Mrs. Peabody spoke. "Snook, you've had quite a day looking after your friend. Put the mower away, stop whatever you were doing inside and go on home."

"Thank you, ma'am, but I don't have much more in the dining room. Will it be okay if I finish that? I'll come back tomorrow to do the bathroom and finish mowing."

"That sounds like a good idea. And I want you to take the Packard so you can go to the hospital in Garland and check on Maddie. You can tell me how he is tomorrow."

"Yes, ma'am. Thank you, ma'am."

Uncle Jasper

"Jasper's awful quiet this evening. He looks like death warmed over. Says his back hurts." I overheard Aunt Fritzie talking to Aunt Geraldine in the kitchen while they washed and dried dishes from our Saturday night dinner at Grandma Dickey's. I didn't intend to eavesdrop. I was on the back porch cooling off because September was hotter than blazes.

"It's a welcome change from his usual smart-alecky self. He thinks he's better than the rest of us. A job in the bank don't make him second in command to God." That was Aunt Geraldine.

"He usually makes a fuss over Laney, but he hasn't gone near her all evening," Aunt Fritzie said. "I wonder if Judy's catching on."

Laney is my mama. Geraldine, Fritzie and Judy are Mama's sisters. I moved nearer to the window.

"Jasper's after every skirt in town—thinks he's God's gift to women." Aunt Geraldine muttered, "Jasper the jackass." She talked like that sometimes when she thought Grandma and us kids were out of earshot.

"I've told Judy over and over she ought to lower the boom on that tomcat right where it would do the most good." Aunt Fritzie snorted and giggled at the same time.

"Well, I'm glad to see him giving Laney some peace." I heard more muttering and caught "son of." I knew the rest of that one.

I could've told them Uncle Jasper wouldn't be bothering Mama anymore.

That morning I sat up in the cool shade of the live oak tree in our backyard, reading a book. I usually go to Grandma Dickey's on Saturday mornings to set the table and help with whatever she's decided on for dessert, but today she'd told me Aunt Judy wanted to help.

"Go on to the library, honey," Grandma said. "Enjoy your day off."

Enjoying my day off is what I was doing when Uncle Jasper came up on the back steps. I didn't see him until he rapped on the screen door.

"Hi, Laney," he called. "I've come to see if there's anything you need around the place."

When there was no answer, he glanced around furtively, a word I'd learned recently, then opened the screen door and went inside. I knew Mama was in the front room sewing and couldn't hear him because the treadle rattled like everything. I climbed out of the tree and went into the kitchen. Jasper was in the front room.

"Jasper! You nearly scared me to death." Mama told him.

"Aw, come on now, Laney. You don't need to be afraid of me. I came by to see if you got something that needs doing? Something a man can do for you?"

When I reached the door to the front room, I saw him put his hand on Mama's cheek. She jumped up, and the chair clattered to the floor. I could tell she was afraid, but she was angry too.

"I've told you before, Jasper, I don't need you to do anything for me. Not anything!"

When he grabbed her by the arm and bent down to kiss her on the mouth, I exploded. I ran into the room and pushed with both hands as hard as I could, knocking him away from Mama. He landed flat on his back.

"You little bitch," he snarled at me. "What are you doing here? You're supposed to be at Grandma Dickey's."

Mama caught hold of me and backed up against the sewing machine. She crossed her arms over my chest because she realized I planned to jump right in the middle of him. He groaned, rolled over and picked himself up. Finally, able to stand, he stooped holding his back.

I thought he'd head for the front door, but no, all of a sudden that varmint came toward us, growling and spitting like a mangy dog. I stood in front of Mama, not moving when she tried to push me out of harm's way. I braced myself against her and raised my right knee. Buddy Longmire once told me a hard kick in the shin can make a grown man cry. Uncle Jasper saw what I had in mind, and he lost his balance. His body weight propelled him helplessly, and he fell toward us. His crotch landed hard on my upraised oxford toe.

Uncle Jasper was on the floor again, doubled up, moaning and groaning. He used curse words I'd never heard. Mama and I stood there, too scared to do anything. When he finally stood up, Uncle Jasper lurched across the room and jerked open the front door. Holding on to the doorjamb, he turned around.

"If you tell anybody about this, I'll, I'll ..." He winced in pain. "Bitches!" He stumbled out to the porch. Mama locked the door. We ran to the kitchen, and she locked the back door too. Mama covered her face with her hands, and her shoulders began to shake. I thought she was crying until she began to laugh and tears rolled down her cheeks.

"Annie, you beat everything. What made you do that?"

I smiled and shrugged my shoulders. She gave me a hug.

"Does your foot hurt?"

"Not much."

"How's your ankle?"

"It's okay."

Uncle Jasper gunned his coupe out of the driveway and down the county road. Mama soaked my foot in warm water and Epsom salts.

Memories

J.C. finished reading the obituary for Marnie Baker Lee, folded the newspaper and placed it on the table next to the large lounge chair. He moved the position of the chair to a medium slant in case he fell asleep. That happened often.

Today J.C. didn't sleep. The memories kept him awake. He smiled when he recalled a day when he and Marnie played their favorite indoor game. They called it house. The linoleum rug in J.C.'s mother's living room had squares with flowers in each space. A narrow stripe separated the squares and in their young minds, it became a neighborhood. Imaginary houses occupied several squares that became rooms. Other squares were yards and streets.

When the new Sears, Roebuck and Montgomery Ward catalogs arrived, J.C. and Marnie cut out families from the clothing section, furniture and appliances from the back pages. They used their small toy cars to take the families to church and shopping at designated squares. Numerous children played outdoors in a park and went to school. With so much imagination, the flowers on the linoleum disappeared. J.C. chuckled. At the time, he was probably eight and Marnie was a year older, but the memory was clear. Even at that young age, J.C. thought he and Marnie would live in a house together someday and go to church with their children.

Another favorite game was the car. It required two wooden produce boxes placed on the grass in the backyard with enough room for their legs to fit when they sat on the rear one. They shoved a stick into the ground for shifting gears. Two pieces of cardboard served as the clutch and brake. They took turns driving and making the necessary sounds. Ayoogah was the horn and loud humming was the smooth-running motor. There were imaginary stops all along the way. "Ayoogah," J.C. whispered.

In patches of dirt their dads had left grassless, they played stick-up with small pocket knives they flipped into the soft earth. Marnie liked to play hopscotch, but J.C. refused to play a girl's game. He watched when Marnie made mud pies in her play dishes.

One day they got into trouble doing what seemed like a good idea. The houses they lived in were built on creosote pilings about two feet off the ground. They noticed that grass had grown up around the pilings, out of reach of their dads' lawnmowers. J.C. got some matches that would strike on a hard surface. When J.C.'s mother found them trying to burn away the grass from the pilings, she almost fainted. Needless to say, the lesson was indelible.

After they started school, J.C. tried to walk with Marnie as many mornings as possible. If the girls in the neighborhood walked together, he'd hang back. J.C. was shy and going to school didn't help. When the children realized his affliction, they teased him. He protected himself by ignoring it. Marnie never teased him, but by third grade he felt like he had become invisible to her.

In high school, J.C. practiced how to ask her to go to the movie or the drug store for a banana split. The conversations never got that far. He gave up when he saw Mike Lee walking her home and taking her places when he learned to drive.

J.C. went to college, came home and opened his own accounting business. He still lived in his childhood home. His parents were dead and his sister lived in another state. Being an uncle gave him great pleasure.

Marnie and Mike went to college, and Mike went into the army out of ROTC. He and Marnie married, raising their family on various army posts. They never returned to the hometown except to visit. The obituary mentioned that Mike survived Marnie. J.C. closed his eyes. Tears slid down his cheeks.

Prairie Life

Home was the sod house Great Grandpa Nason built when he bought prairie land from the railroad in 1890. The original house was built into the side of a small hill. Some year's later, Grandpa Nason added a front room and a second bedroom with windows. A narrow porch with a sloping roof ran across the front and kept out summer's harsh sun and winter's heavy snow.

Grandpa and Grandma Nason had the front bedroom. We slept in the room under the hill. There were no windows, but it was cool in summer and warm in winter. Mama and Daddy's bed was a wooden shelf with a cornhusk mattress. Extra clothes were stored in the space underneath. Our everyday clothes hung on pegs. Luther, Gladys and I slept on the floor. When our baby sister, Mary, was born, Daddy made a cradle that fit into the niche at the head of their sleeping shelf.

Doolie, our uncle, had a lean-to on the south side of the barn. The inside walls were covered with animal hides for insulation. Additional warmth came from his big dog, Chosen, who had a thick coat and looked like a bear until he moved.

Before the Great War, four Nason brothers worked the farm with their father. In spring 1917, Jace, Cole and Doolie signed up to fight. Daddy was too young to enlist. Doolie came back alone. Physically unwounded, he lived in another world. Daddy told us the war replaced the twinkle in his blue eyes with the dull stare we saw. Doolie's soft voice was almost a whisper. He answered questions with as few words as needed and never spoke unless we spoke to him. Our grandmother, Maude, was sharp with everyone except Doolie. He got the best meat and the most cake. He never looked at her or smiled.

Daddy met our mother, Anna Reitenbusch, at a church social when she was eighteen. He was twenty-one. A year later, they married and moved into the sod house. Grandma Maude didn't find out Mama was part Indian until after I was born. Grandma Reitenbusch was Ute but had been adopted by a white missionary family when her parents died in a smallpox epidemic. They named her Adele and she never knew her Native American family. She married Adolf Reitenbusch, a farmer, our grandfather.

Grandma Nason made our lives miserable, calling Mama an "Indian slut," and telling Daddy he was "good for nuthin." She yelled at us kids for the least thing and called us "half-breeds." I've wondered since, if the harshness of life on a poor farm out in the middle of nowhere and the grief of losing her sons, especially Doolie, destroyed the person she might have been at one time.

One evening, Luther, Gladys and I were sitting at the table doing homework. Grandma came in from the kitchen. She began yelling at Gladys, saying she was a dumb Injun like her mother and didn't know how to wash dirty dishes. Gladys jumped up from her chair, scared to death. Grandma swung and slapped Gladys across her cheek. Our small sister fell to the floor, blood running down the side of her face.

Mama heard the ruckus and came running from the bedroom. "You bitch," she screamed. I thought she was going to hit Grandma, but she fell on her knees and began tending Gladys. Daddy came in from outdoors and realized what had happened. I went to the kitchen and returned with a wet dishcloth to clean the blood from our sister's face. After a while, Gladys seemed to be herself, just shaky. Mama and Daddy put us to bed. We didn't go to sleep for a long time because of the angry voices coming from the next room.

We left the next day, a frosty April morning. The wagon easily held our few belongings. I was ten, Luther was eight and Gladys was almost six. Mary was four months old. Grandma stood on the porch with a frown on her face and hands on her hips. Grandpa and Doolie were down in the field. Though no one said anything, I knew all of us were glad to be leaving.

After we'd gone a way, we began singing songs Mama taught us when Grandma wasn't around. Daddy put his arm around Mama. Mary didn't cry a bit. The sun warmed us and the wind was gentle. Alongside a creek with trees starting to leaf out, we ate the lunch Mama fixed. Daddy said there might be snakes in the tall grass, so we stayed close by.

Toward sunset, Daddy pulled the wagon up to a wooden farmhouse surrounded by packed dirt and a few hardy weeds growing in neglected flowerbeds. Smoke rose from a stone chimney. I hoped that was a good sign. Tired and hungry, I wondered what waited for us behind those walls.

The door opened, and a short man, almost as wide as he was tall, stepped out onto the porch. Grandpa Reitenbusch was compact, not fat. A dingy, plaid coat covered his shoulders and hung past his hips.

Heavy legs ended in work-worn boots laced to his knees. He wore a wide-brimmed felt hat whose original color was lost in time. Bushy gray eyebrows grew across a weathered forehead. He had a heavy nose, a gray mustache and beard. His arms crossed over a barrel chest. No greeting. No smile. Later, we saw eyes as blue as a mountain lake.

When we got into the wagon the day before, I thought all of us were leaving never to return. The next morning, it was hard not to cry as we watched our father switch the old mule down the trace on his way back to Grandma and Grandpa Nason.

Mama and us kids soon settled into life with Grandpa and Uncle August, who had been a medic in the Great War. Sometimes he got that same far-off look like Doolie. He would disappear and return in a day or two as though nothing had happened. Grandpa Reitenbusch never seemed to notice. Uncle August slept in a small room inside the barn. It was more substantial than Doolie's lean-to and had a kerosene heater. A big, skinny hound slept at his feet. Uncle August called him Dog.

Grandpa grumped loudly when his daughter ordered him out of the house. We cleaned it top to bottom. The main room where we cooked, ate and sat in the evening, was cluttered, dirty and full of cobwebs. The rock fireplace was a sooty mess. You could hardly see out of the small windowpanes until we cleaned them inside and out. Mama had Luther and me lugging buckets of water and scrubbing as hard as she did. Gladys took care of Mary. Grandpa didn't want us in his bedroom, but Mama threatened to pour out all his schnapps. The smaller room, in which we slept, was almost bare and easier to clean. There was a narrow bed and shelves on one wall for our things. Within a week, Uncle August built a three-tiered bunk bed. It wasn't fancy but built to last. Later he made a small bed for Mary. It would last too.

Through the years, our grandpa and uncle had made all the furniture in the house. It was plain and utilitarian, except for two pieces Grandma Reitenbusch brought on her wedding day. An etagere held crystal, ceramic and pewter items. A slender, armless rocking chair had a woven reed seat. Five round spindles formed the back, held by a slightly curved headpiece on which a rose was carved. Like her mother, our mother sat there sewing or reading.

When we arrived, Uncle August was doing all the farm chores. Grandpa had rheumatism and could help sometimes, but mostly it all fell on his son. Our uncle cared for six cows, two pigs, some chickens, two mules and two horses. We watched him do his chores, and he didn't seem to mind our being there. We were careful to stay out of his way. One evening when he was milking, he offered us a cup of warm milk. I wanted to milk a cow right then but thought I'd better get to know my uncle better.

We had been living with Grandpa Reitenbusch for about a week when I realized how different things were. There was no screaming and name-calling. Mama worked hard, but she smiled a lot. Mary cried less. Luther, Gladys and I explored the entire farm, climbed trees in the pasture and fished in the creek. No one ever yelled at us.

There was a routine, and everyone had a place in it. As it turned out, Luther and I learned to do all the farm chores and eventually became responsible for keeping the place going. Though we worked harder than ever before, it gave us a sense of worth and assurance. Grandpa Reitenbusch didn't say it, but we knew he liked having us there. One day he took Luther and me into his bedroom. A large cabinet with glass-paned doors held books which he allowed us to take down and look at. Most were English, but some were in German and a few in French and Spanish. Mama told us later that Grandma Reitenbusch's missionary parents had given them to her as she grew up.

"Ask your mama. She help you find good books," he said.

After that, Mama read to us before we went to bed. She also taught our lessons since the nearest school was too far away. One night we asked our mother when Daddy was coming. We didn't want to return to Grandpa Nason's, but we missed our daddy. "One of these days," she said and gave us a kiss.

Uncle August planted wheat and corn, walking behind the mules from sunrise to sunset. Before long, I was helping. Luther and Gladys worked the soil where our grandmother had gardened. It was near the porch and caught sun all day. When the vegetables started coming up, we took turns watering, weeding and watching for rabbits. One day, Uncle August brought a trap he'd made and set it up in the garden. Mama served some delicious stews.

After a while, Grandpa and Mama visited in the evening. We discovered our mother spoke German when she didn't want us to know what they talked about. Grandpa had a heavy accent, making his English hard to understand. I wondered if that was why he said so little. Though he rarely spoke to us, he began patting us on the head or shoulder and smiling. His blue eyes were warm. Mama told us he'd come from Germany as a child. Like many, he went to work on the family farm and never attended an American school. Our grandmother taught him to read and write English after they were married.

Uncle August made benches for the front porch where we sometimes sat in the evening, enjoying the prairie breeze and watching glorious sunsets. Mama knew the names for all the unusual colors as well as the clouds. One evening, our uncle took a small harmonica out of his pocket and began to play, "Down in the valley, valley so low ..." He played many tunes, some I'd never heard before or since. I think he made them up.

Although we missed our daddy, we were happy for the first time in our short lives. It was almost too good to be true. I suppressed an ominous feeling before I went to sleep.

One night, Mama was putting us to bed, and Uncle August and Grandpa Reitenbusch were having their schnapps. We heard horses coming. Too late for neighbors to visit. Mama left our room and closed the door. Luther and I got out of our bunks and opened it a crack. Grandpa stood behind the dining table, his large pistol at his side. There were two loud raps.

"Who comes?" Grandpa called. Uncle August took his hunting rifle down from the rack over the fireplace.

"Jonathan Nason, sir."

"Open," Grandpa said to our uncle, who pulled the cross latch and opened the heavy wooden door. Our father stood there, dusty and weary. He took off his wide-brimmed hat and walked into the room toward our mother, smiling. I saw Doolie just outside the door.

"Anna, I've come to take you and the children home for good," our daddy said.

"No!" Uncle August shouted and raised his rifle. The sound of a gunshot reverberated in the small room. Our father fell to the floor. Blood ran from the back of his head. Mama screamed and threw herself across his still body. Luther and I stood frozen in disbelief.

Doolie dropped to one knee, raised his rifle to his shoulder and fired through the open door. Uncle August fell forward. Blood covered the back of his shirt. Grandpa Reitenbusch aimed his pistol and shot Doolie between the eyes.

About that time, we heard Grandpa Nason cursing. He came into the room with his rifle cocked. Grandpa Reitenbusch shot him too. The old man dropped his gun and fell, screaming curses. He was not mortally wounded.

An inquest found Grandpa Reitenbusch not guilty by reason of self-defense. Pastor Andersen held the funeral down in the pasture inside a fenced area. We buried our daddy and Uncle August at Grandma Reitenbusch's feet. Doolie was laid on the far side of the cemetery, in a corner away from the others.

After the funeral, Grandpa stayed down in the cemetery until dark. When he came into the house, we saw he was different. He had the same faraway look of Doolie and Uncle August. When Mama put his dinner on the table, she had to guide him to his chair. He ate a few bites and went into his room.

Grandma Maude had died of a stroke in the midst of a tantrum. Daddy had planned to bring us back to live on the farm he and Doolie would inherit. Instead, our Grandpa Nason returned to his farm alone. He died soon after. The house and property were mortgaged to the limit, and the bank foreclosed.

We lived on the farm with Grandpa Reitenbusch who went through the motions of living but wasn't there anymore. Occasionally, he would pat us as before, but there was no smile. He'd sit for the longest, watching Mary sleep in her cradle. Mama hid his pistol and Uncle August's rifle.

Neighbors helped us finish getting in the crops and prepare for winter. Luther, Gladys and I worked harder than ever. We missed Uncle August and his songs. Mama grieved Daddy and tried not to let us see her crying. Luther, Gladys and I cried ourselves to sleep every night. Just before Thanksgiving, Grandpa found his pistol.

We stayed in spite of that terrible evening when we lost our daddy, and two uncles and then the grandpa we'd grown to love. It felt like home, and we had no other place to go. Fortunately, Grandpa's legal matters were in order. Through the winter, Luther, Gladys and I did all the farm chores. That next spring several of the neighbors came over and helped Luther and me plow and sow wheat and corn. Mama managed to hire help as the Great Depression came on and men were looking for work that gave them food to eat and a place to sleep.

Times were hard, but our mother kept us fed, clothed and schooled. We all looked after Mary. Though Mama was exhausted at night, she read to us, sang with us and hugged us before we went to bed. After a while, we didn't cry every night, just sometimes.

Thomas Olson came into our lives two years later. He was a good man who worked hard and loved our mother. It was a glorious day when they married. We called him Dad.

River of Escape

Dom pushed his pirogue away from the levee and decided it would be the last time. Making his way past creosote pilings of a shipping wharf, he observed a dirty, medium-sized cargo ship coming toward the pier to take on a load of sulphur. The dock crew, standing at the ready, returned his wave. Dom watched the ship tie up.

From the storage yard on shore, where freshly mined sulphur lay in large yellow chunks, a pair of immense bucket-like tongs suspended from a steel girder moved back and forth, scooping up piles of the mineral and dropping them onto a conveyer belt. The yellow mounds traveled through corrugated housing to the docked ship where they fell from the belt into the cargo hold.

A yellow, acrid dust enveloped the yard and ship. Sometimes fires ignited in the yard and were extinguished with large hoses spouting gallons of water. At one time, Dom watched for those fires, sounded the alarm and directed the hose operator to hot spots. In twenty years, there had never been an uncontrolled fire on Dom's shift.

Workmen at the yard and the ship's crew wore goggles to keep their eyes from burning. They breathed in the dust without concern since there was little sensation of burning in their throats or lungs. Eventually, Dom could no longer breathe deeply without discomfort. Crashing headaches came on suddenly. The company sent him to doctors in New Orleans.

"We can find nothing wrong," the doctors said, while writing out another prescription for pain.

"Bellyachin' Cajun," said Dom's wife, Jolie.

Sometimes he felt better, but then he collapsed and was unable to work for days. Finally, the company retired him with a monthly disability check.

"Now, you jus like dem other lazy Cajuns," said Jolie. "I never expect dis." She soon found work cleaning houses.

Though he tried, Dom wasn't able to hold other jobs, menial and low-paying, for any length of time. He lost consciousness because of the pain in his chest, and the blinding headaches kept him in bed for days at a time. Finally, he gave up. With the small check he received from the company and Jolie's modest income, they were able to keep their humble home behind the levee on the west bank of the river. Dom fished and hunted to supplement the groceries and discovered his green thumb in a small, bountiful garden.

After a couple of years, he thought Jolie was beginning to understand the truth of his disability because she hadn't lashed out at him in a long time. Dom said to her that morning, "You know, chère, when I'm out fishing or hunting, dat pain she goes away."

"Nuttin wrong wit you, Dom," his wife said. "You just got yourself a way to hunt and fish when you please." Dom's stomach churned. He wanted to grab her and slap her smart mouth. Show her a thing or two. But, he didn't. Jolie was as tall as he, and now she was stronger. She would have knocked the crap out of him or called the sheriff. Or both, he thought. She curled her lip and slammed the door when she left the house.

Dom spit tobacco juice into the murky water as he dug his paddle deeper. Soon the pirogue hit the main current of the river where he rested the paddle and drifted. The river was almost a mile wide. There was no sign of human habitation on the east bank. Marsh grass and stunted trees grew, constantly abraded by the river's salty tide because there was no levee.

When Dom got to a certain point and saw the low narrow wharf, he turned the small craft eastward. Strong currents challenged him, and he dodged several eddies but was finally able to cut a straight course for the east bank. He loved maneuvering the pirogue he had carved out so many years ago.

Dom constructed the crude wharf from varied widths and lengths of wood. The idea came to him one day when he was out on the river, and an ocean liner cruised toward the Gulf of Mexico. Dom saw the ship coming and knew he couldn't get back to the levee, but he made it out of the liner's path. Rolling waves in the ship's wake spun and pitched the pirogue precariously. Dom skillfully kept it from overturning, but the turbulent water tossed him and his craft up onto the grass-covered east bank. Passengers on the decks recognized his expert handling of the pirogue and waved when they saw him safely beached. Dom waved back. Pride brought a smile to his face.

"Some tings dis ole Cajun can still do."

The liner's wake continued to wash up on him and the pirogue, sending scraps of lumber onto the grass beside him. Dom looked around and saw more pieces lying on the bank. He cached them far from the water and on his return the next day brought tools to build the wharf. On another trip, he toted boards he'd scavenged around town. Pieces of scrap lumber continued to wash up.

One day, Dom looked up at the clear sky and grinned. "Hey, God, is dis some of dat manna I hear about?"

Before long, Dom had a wharf about four feet wide, extending twenty feet into the grass and bushes. He didn't put up handrails because he didn't want it to be visible from the west side of the river. Don't need no company, he thought.

Dom wasn't sure why he wanted to build a wharf, but it felt good. He liked to stretch out on a sunny day, take a nap. Some days he sat and waved to the ships. His chest hadn't bothered him at any time during the construction nor had he suffered any headaches. Maybe I build me a shack, he thought, and den Jolie, she can worry when I don't show up ever night. He never built the shack.

Today, when he reached the wharf, he was still wounded by Jolie's sarcasm and callousness. Dat woman got no feelins except fo herself, he thought. She don't care if I never come back.

Dom got out of the pirogue, but instead of tying it to the wharf, he turned it out toward the river, paused for a moment and gave it a hard shove. It drifted close to the bank for a while and then, as he expected, the craft hit an eddy that spun it around and out into the current. The pirogue bounced along, smaller and smaller.

"Too bad I haf to let you go. But I got no mo use fo a pirogue."

Dom turned toward the wharf with tears in his eyes. He took the hunting knife from his belt scabbard and began to hack at the boards. Dom continued his savage attack, and the planks started to give. Soon the wharf was again a collection of odd lumber that he threw out into the river with what strength he had left. Eddies caught the scraps and eventually they either sank or bobbled in the current. He threw his knife after them.

Dom sobbed and gasped for breath, his chest burning as though a fiery ball ricocheted from one wall to the other. His head throbbed and his sight blurred. Dom stepped into the river, brought a dripping hand to his forehead and continued to make the sign of the cross before he swam out to join the gulf bound current.

"That was quick, Darlene. Thank you." Darlene did not reply or turn her head.

Suzanne made a right turn out of Homestead Park and drove to the freeway entrance ramp. Commuter car lights beamed toward them. Daylight broke behind them.

Suzanne looked over at Darlene and reached to pull her black hood forward until it hid the woman's dark hair and her classic profile. Suzanne glanced in the mirror to be sure the knit cap hid her own blonde bob. She pushed wire-rimmed glasses up on her nose. Neither wore makeup.

"Nondescript. That's us, Darlene." There was only silence from the inscrutable passenger.

An hour later, Suzanne exited the freeway slowing to navigate a potholed road that rose sharply and zigzagged through a dense forest. After a steep climb of two miles, the ground leveled off, and she turned onto a narrow dirt road. A sign said, "No Trespassing." After more curves through thick woods, Suzanne stopped at a solid iron gate set in a ten-foot high masonry wall, topped with embedded glass and barbed wire. A small sign warned of an electric security system. Suzanne pressed a button on the car's visor. The narrow gate swung inward and then clanged shut as soon as they were clear.

"That sound always makes me feel good," Suzanne said, glancing at her passenger who looked straight ahead. A paved drive wound through a canopy of tall trees and heavy brush. After a ninety degree turn, Suzanne drove into a clearing, toward a brick ranch style house, landscaped with a mowed lawn and low shrubs. No flowers.

She drove around to the back toward an attached double garage. When she pressed a second button on the visor, the door farthest from the house opened. As soon as the station wagon was inside, the door closed. Fluorescent tubes lit up the windowless enclosure. The other garage space was walled off, accessible through a metal panel.

"We made it, Darlene."

Suzanne touched three buttons on the visor, causing all four car doors and the tailgate to open. She took a small cartridge from her jacket pocket, pushed a series of buttons, watching as a motorized chair traveled from the front of the garage to her open door. After maneuvering herself into the chair, Suzanne rode to the metal panel leading into the walled-off section of the garage.

"Darlene. Listen." Suzanne said, in a measured cadence. "Come, stand behind my chair. When I move, you follow." Darlene got out of the car, stood behind the motorized chair. In response to Suzanne entering a series of numbers into a mounted keypad, the metal panel slid into the wall. Darlene followed as Suzanne guided her chair into the room. Once they were clear, the panel slid shut. Suzanne pulled a lever on the wall. A splashing, humming noise came from the garage. In ten minutes the car would be spotless, inside and out. Both car and garage would be dry.

Darlene followed as Suzanne drove her chair around a laboratory furnished with stainless steel cabinets, shelves, counters and a large table in the center. Microscopes, racks of tubes, vials and all the necessary equipment were neatly arranged, ready for use.

Suzanne reached into a drawer and retrieved a plastic bag. She held it open.

"Darlene. Listen. Remove your poncho. Drop the poncho into the bag." Darlene did so. Then, she stood before Suzanne in a black sweatshirt, black jeans and black sneakers that were bloody, muddy, and flecked with grass and small twigs. Dirt smudged her face.

"Darlene. Listen. Give me the knife." Darlene pulled a bloody ten-inch carving knife out of the hand warmer pocket and handed it to Suzanne.

In a far corner stood a tall three-sided built-in shower. Frosted glass formed the door and top.

"Darlene. Listen. Enter the shower. Close the door."

Darlene complied. Suzanne selected three rocker switches on the wall next to the shower: WASH GENTLE. DRY GENTLE. START. Sounds, similar to a washing machine, came from the enclosure.

Suzanne moved over to a counter and opened a container that looked like a stainless steel bread box. She placed the bloody knife inside and pushed a button. After three minutes of soft whirring, a small panel under the button lit up. CLEAN. She placed the spotless knife in a drawer that contained an assortment of sharp, gleaming cutlery.

Above the counter, Suzanne opened what looked like a kitchen oven without a window. She placed the bag containing Darlene's poncho inside and pulled a lever next to the door. When a beep sounded five minutes later, she nodded in satisfaction at the clean, empty interior.

Turning to a sink in the table, Suzanne washed a few traces of blood from her hands, sprayed disinfectant into the basin and scrubbed it thoroughly. Straight blonde hair fell to her shoulders when she removed the knit cap. She dropped the hat and her wire-rimmed glasses into a drawer.

The sounds in the shower shut off. When the door opened, a faint odor of lavender wafted into the room.

"Darlene. Listen. Come stand in front of me." The tall young woman walked toward Suzanne wearing dry, clean clothes and sneakers. All signs of dirt and blood were gone from her face and hands.

"Darlene. Listen. Kneel and look at me." Suzanne dabbed the upturned face with a soft towel, checked hands and fingernails. "Perfect," she said. "Darlene. Listen. Turn around slowly while I brush your hair." Soon Darlene's head was a crown of soft brown curls.

"Darlene. Listen. Give me the camera." Darlene opened her mouth, made a clicking sound. A small camera appeared on her tongue. Suzanne took it and placed it in a drawer. "We'll review this later," she said.

"Darlene. Listen. Stand behind my chair and follow me." They moved to a door where Suzanne pressed numbers on a keypad. The women entered a kitchen. On a wall of maple cabinet doors and drawers, Suzanne touched a series of white, enamel knobs. A tall section of drawers swung out, revealing a closet whose interior was a dull stainless steel. An overstuffed armchair, upholstered in navy blue velvet, sat in the center.

"Darlene, Listen. Enter your room. Sit in your chair. Rest. Thank you." Darlene stepped into the closet, sat down and closed her eyes. Suzanne touched the white knobs. The wall of drawers swung back into place.

Suzanne moved around a kitchen designed for her disabilities. She ate a breakfast of scrambled eggs, English muffins and coffee while looking out the window onto a well-kept yard. Small birds flew to and from several feeders. Suzanne looked at her watch and picked up a television remote.

"Police found a man about an hour ago at the bottom of the ravine that runs through Homestead Park. No name has been released, but police say he is between thirty and forty years old. Joggers on the nearby trail heard weak cries but were unable to see anyone because of the depth of the ravine and the thick growth of trees and shrubs. Police believe the victim was assaulted on the trail and his body hurled into the creek below. By the time the rescue crew located him, he was unconscious. The attacker stabbed him brutally numerous times but seemed to avoid killing him. His condition is critical." There was a pause before the newscaster continued. "This has always been a dangerous place for solo hikers and joggers. Exactly five years ago this month, there was a particularly brutal attack on a female jogger. An engineering student at Johnson Technical Institute almost died from the injuries she suffered. Her assailant was never captured, though the police identified a person of interest at one time."

Suzanne nodded and sipped her coffee.

When Things Go Bump in the Night

Jim's eyes flew open, his heart pounded. It was pitch dark in the bedroom.

"What the ...?" He shook himself, then realized he had been asleep when three loud thumps against the side of the house awoke him. Each thump had been a demanding one. Just like Margot thumped the wall above their bed when he snored loudly. "Wish it were you, Honey," he said.

Jim knew it was the Monterey Cypress that was encroaching on the house, but he had put off the annual pruning while Margot was so sick those last months. "You loved that tree and would have been out supervising. It was your tree. It's still your tree." He chuckled.

Jim was wide awake and as always, his first thoughts were of his wife. Remembering. Just eleven days and I miss you more than ever. He decided to get up and go upstairs to the kitchen. Some Bud might taste good.

He didn't have to turn on any lights. She had put a night light in the downstairs hallway, one at the top of the stairs and another at the far side of the kitchen. "So, you won't break something I love, especially you, when you're creeping around at night," she had teased. The fourth stair creaked and reminded him that Margot wouldn't let him fix it because she could hear him if he got up in the night. Now he stepped on it twice. "I won't fix it, Honey. Ever."

The upstairs was an open room. The kitchen and living area looked out through large windows toward the ocean. Tonight, a full moon made it seem almost like daylight. He walked across the room, slid open the glass door and stepped out onto the deck. The moon's light sparkled on the moving water, mixing gold and silver with the foamy white crest of the waves. Tall trees cast shadows across the road.

"Our favorite sound," Jim murmured. "Remember how we stayed up all night the first time in our new home? I love to hear the rocks clatter as the water backs away. You do too. Wherever you are."

Jim stood on the deck until the coolness began to penetrate his cotton robe. He got a Bud from the fridge and decided to sit in his lounge chair, pushing the recline button. He clicked the television remote and found the music channels. Big band was his favorite.

"Remember the time Tommy Dorsey came to the university for the spring prom? We danced and danced. I remember how beautiful you were in the blue lace dress with no straps. I remember your long blonde hair, brown eyes. I loved the way you hummed every tune."

Jim finished the drink and closed his eyes. "I love you, Margot." The music played on as he slept. Gentle humming came from the empty lounge chair beside his.

Scattered Flowers

The gray-flecked hair made Marsh look older than his thirty-three years. Slender, six feet two, he didn't carry his height with the sureness of most tall men. It was as though he didn't want to be tall, to be noticed.

After considering the annual plants arranged on tables in the garden center. he picked up three boxes of bright petunias and placed them in the small red wagon next to his feet. Daisies, marigolds, pansies and one large red geranium waited.

He brushed dirt from his hands onto his jeans. A faded, long-sleeved, green and blue plaid cotton shirt was tucked in, and a well-worn leather belt ran through the loops. His dusty loafers looked comfortable. Blue eyes sat deep in an ordinary face over a nose that had a slight but noticeable zigzag in the bridge. Thin lips looked as though they rarely smiled.

Marsh moved on, stooping to reach the wagon handle. Suddenly he stumbled, tipping the wagon over and strewing the plants on the gray, gravel walkway. Trying to keep his balance, he couldn't avoid stepping on the blooms and causing more damage.

"Oh, no," he whispered, staring at the broken flowers scattered over the gray gravel. Red petals, torn from the geranium stems looked like large drops of blood. Twisted marigolds and pansies held crushed, colorful blooms spattered with potting soil. White daisies lay sprinkled among scattered petunias.

Memory filled him with a cold numbness. No one noticed as he left the garden center and got into an older American station wagon. He sat for a few minutes before driving slowly out of the parking lot. Sometime later he turned into a fast food drive-through.

"Taco with hot sauce and a large root beer," he said into the microphone.

After paying, he turned into the thoroughfare once again and drove to the nearby lakefront. He parked so that he could watch the fishermen dropping their lines from a pier. Sailboats moving across the water reminded him of the carefree days he spent here with Rita and the little girls, Gina and Marie. A year ago, he sobbed when he sat here. Today, there was only numbness. Would he get over it? He hoped not. Finishing the drink, he stuffed the uneaten taco into the cup and dropped it on the floor of the car.

Marsh was a high school teacher when Rita and the girls went away. Now he worked as an evening security guard for a small manufacturing plant outside town. The hours kept him out of the apartment in the evenings and most of the night. After his shift, he slept from 4 AM to 10 AM, if he slept at all. After daily survival chores, he was out and about until time to go to work. That day, he went to the garden center on impulse, wanting to put flowers in the planters on his balcony. He never would now.

As he turned into the parking lot of the apartment complex where he lived, he saw Jason, a downstairs neighbor, hosing off his car. Marsh returned the wave and pulled into his designated parking space.

"Hey, Marsh." Jason motioned to him.

Groaning under his breath, Marsh ambled over. He always resisted Jason's efforts to establish more than a distant friendliness.

"Hey, buddy. How's it going?" Jason grinned broadly.

"Nowhere." Marsh tried to sound relaxed.

"Always the optimist," laughed Jason. "That's what I like about you." He paused to turn off the hose before continuing. "Some of the guys are coming over for pizza, beer and poker tonight. I'd like to have you join us. Good bunch, no rowdies, just goofballs like me."

Marsh smiled at the good humor. This was his night off when he usually went to a movie and stayed through the last showing. "I'll see," he replied with a smile so Jason would know he appreciated the invitation. Marsh recognized that the younger man tried to get through to him without being intrusive, but he wasn't able to lower the wall he lived behind. Not yet. Marsh climbed the stairs to his apartment, turned on the television and flopped on the couch. He wanted to shut out the scene of broken, colorful flowers scattered over gray gravel in the garden center.

Marsh hadn't always lived behind a wall. He, too, had been friendly and outgoing. He liked being with people, especially young people, which explained his becoming a teacher. After he met Rita, life had taken on a golden quality he couldn't believe at times. When she agreed to marry him, he thought life would never be better. The little girls came along, and it got better than ever. Most evenings, he and Rita cuddled on the couch after the girls' bedtime, talking, exchanging kisses and caresses. He moaned softly at the memory.

A year ago, that life evaporated like morning fog on a sunny day. A year ago, an airliner crashed into a craggy mountainside. The pictures in the newscasts showed debris that looked like broken, colorful flowers scattered over gray gravel.

Marsh looked at the photograph he kept on the coffee table. Rita, Gina and Marie smiled at him. He always spent time looking at his beautiful ones, often talking to them. Today, something seemed different in the way they smiled at him. After several minutes. he picked up the photo and held it to his chest.

"You're right. I'll try."

A loud banging on the door stirred him.

"Hey, Marsh. I came to check on you." It was his friendly downstairs neighbor.

"We're getting started and need you to fill out the table," Jason announced as he and a tall friend, both grinning, stepped into the entry. Marsh started to make an excuse but found himself being carefully but firmly guided out the door and down the stairs. Both Jason and his friend were talking at the top of their voices and laughing raucously. Marsh smelled beer.

"We got him. We got him. Now the games can begin," they chanted.

Contrary to his inclination, Marsh allowed himself to be propelled into Jason's apartment. Three young men were in the kitchen, beer cans in hand. Following introductions, Marsh joined in eating a slice of pizza, washing it down with Bud. The five seemed to be friends of long standing so Marsh didn't have to say much beyond an occasional "yeah" and "that so?" Escape was out of the question as he moved with the group into the living room toward a round table set up for poker.

"I don't know what kind of a poker player we have here," Jason said.

"No kind," Marsh said.

"Still the optimist," Jason laughed loudly.

True to his earlier comment, Jason's friends were not rowdies, just a bunch of congenial goofballs. Marsh found himself relaxing and thinking only of how not to lose too much money.

The Visit

"Mom, I'd rather not go with you to visit Grandma Eleanor. I want to remember her like she was. Before I left for college, she'd become forgetful and confused. Now she's in that place, and I don't want to see her going out of her mind."

Shelby sat across the kitchen table from her mother, Carol. In the center was a smiling ceramic Santa Claus standing in a wreath of spruce and holly. Eleanor, Shelby's grandmother, had made it and given it to her daughter, Carol, many years ago. This had been his holiday place since Shelby could remember.

"Your grandmother isn't out of her mind," Carol said. "The dementia is progressing. That is why we placed her where she can get the care she needs. There are days when she recognizes me and remembers recent happenings. Other days, she's in another place, another time." Carol paused. "It isn't easy to see her change, but this is what she's been given—what we who love her have been given—and we must help her through it as best we can."

"Oh, Mom. I just don't know." Shelby shook her head.

"Seeing you may jar her memory or she may have no idea who you are. Don't worry. She doesn't rant and rave or froth at the mouth." Carol's tone had sharpened. "I want to leave in half an hour."

They climbed the back stairs from the kitchen to the second floor bedrooms. Carol took a deep breath to hold back the tears. Shelby said nothing. Thirty minutes later they were on the way to the care center.

"Mom, if it gets to be too much, may I please leave? Kelly, a friend at school, has an aunt who has Alzheimer's, and she's told me some really weird stuff. Once Kelly was going to kiss her aunt goodbye on the cheek, and the woman yelled bloody murder and began calling her terrible names. Kelly started crying while she was telling me."

"Shelby, you're a sensitive young woman, which explains some of your misgivings. Please relax. You'll know the right thing to do." Carol smiled at her.

They reached the care center and signed in at the desk.

"It's good to see you," said a smiling young woman. "Mrs. Lacey is a favorite. Even when she loses her reality, she's a sweetheart." Shelby smiled, but the flutter in her stomach refused to subside.

The attendant unlocked a door and led them down a hallway where each door on either side had the occupant's picture with their name below. A small table sat beside the door with flowers, figurines or other mementos. Shelby assumed all this made it easier for the residents to find their rooms.

When they reached Grandma Eleanor's room, the attendant knocked, opened the door and called out, "Mrs. Lacey?" Shelby's grandmother was standing inside, dressed in a lavender pantsuit with a crisp white blouse. Her makeup was perfect, and she smiled her warm, familiar smile. White curls framed her still beautiful face like a halo. Shelby was surprised to see the large room furnished with pieces from her grandmother's home. Even the drapes had been resized and hung at the windows.

"Oh, Marianne. I'm so glad to see you. It's been such a long time." The small slender woman held her arms out to Carol, who stepped forward and enveloped her mother in a long hug and kissed the smooth cheek.

"Jennifer," Eleanor said, opening her arms for Shelby's hug and kiss. "You were such a little one when I saw you last. You look more like your Aunt Carol than your mother."

Today Eleanor thought Carol and Shelby were the daughter and granddaughter who had died ten years ago in an automobile accident.

"Doreen," Eleanor called to the attendant who was turning to leave. "Don't bring our tea until I ring for it." The young woman, whose name was Martha, smiled. "Of course, Mrs. Lacey."

Carol knew her mother was back to a time when her other daughter and grandchild were still living, They were visiting in the house where Carol and Marianne had grown up. There had been servants, and afternoon tea was Eleanor's favorite time of day, especially when she had guests. Carol smiled at Shelby to reassure her.

"I've been waiting for you to visit me for quite some time, Marianne. Carol hasn't been here for a while either." Carol caught the querulous note in her mother's voice but didn't remind her of last week's visit.

"Mother, your granddaughter is home from Smith for the holidays."

"Oh, yes. I'd forgotten," Eleanor said, chuckling softly. "I was a Smith woman too. What wonderful years they were."

Eleanor began to recollect her years as a college student, reciting friends, their full names, where they were from. The parties and fun were endless. She recounted her four years at Smith in such detail that Carol heard anecdotes from her mother's young life that had never been shared before. Eleanor regaled them with stories of the football games at Yale, Harvard and Brown. World War II came and she met Ensign James Winthrop Lacey.

"He was so handsome," Eleanor said. "It was love at first sight for us, but we had to wait until the war was over. He was in the South Pacific for two years. How I worried."

The older woman paused a moment, then resumed her stories. Shelby and Carol were caught up in the telling, asking questions that prompted more revelations. The three of them laughed at times until tears ran down their cheeks.

"Oh, my dears, I haven't had such a lovely, entertaining afternoon in years. Don't you think we should have tea? I'll ring."

"Why don't you let me see to it, Grandmother? I'll make sure everything is just right."

"I'm sure you will, Shelby."

Watching, Waiting

I still remember the evening when we sat together at the window. Mama, Josie and I were waiting for Daddy to come home from his job.

Daddy and Mama got up early that morning. Josie and I were awake in the small storage room next to the kitchen that was also our bedroom. There was no window, but Mama had put up a rod on the unpainted outer wall and hung a ruffled curtain made from printed flour sacks, covering the entire wall. I realized later that it kept us warmer in that drafty little room which extended from the back of the house. Our narrow bed was made warmer with a spread made of flour sack scraps from which Mama had made our dresses.

We were supposed to be asleep so we stayed where it was warm. The wall was thin, and the door didn't fit good—leaving cracks at the top and the bottom. Mama and Daddy talked low, but we could hear them plain as day.

"I hope Mr. Wiggins will keep his word and give you another chance," Mama said.

"He don't have much choice. I know what I'm doing, and he needs to get this job done."

"Jake you are a smart man and know all about electrical things, but that hasn't kept you working steady. Lord knows we are really scraping the bottom of the barrel again." Mama's tone was soft but I was afraid she was going to rile him.

"Now listen, Serena. Don't start that, I work hard and I work good, but I won't take crap offa nobody. I'm a man, and I'll stand up to anybody." Daddy was getting mad at Mama.

Even though times were hard, Daddy had lots of jobs because he knew about electricity. Still, in six months or so he would be let go. Sometimes we would move to another town where no one had heard of his hair-trigger temper.

Mama worried. They argued. One time he said she better respect her husband like she was supposed to or he wasn't going to put up with her. That scared us, but later Mama said Daddy was under a lot of strain and didn't mean it He never hit Josie or me but he didn't pay us much attention either. "Shoulda been at least one boy," he'd say sometimes when he was having a drink out of his special bottle from the top shelf of the pantry.

We heard the wooden back door slam and the screen slap shut. After a while, we dropped off to sleep until Mama woke us up to go to school. We had grits with dry toast and a glass of milk.

I was tired of grits and longed for bacon and eggs, but we were near the bottom of the barrel so I didn't say anything. When these times came, we ate a lot of red beans and rice, with potatoes, cabbage, onions and greens from Mama's garden. When she could afford the seeds she would plant tomatoes, green beans and carrots We rarely ate red meat—chicken sometimes. At noon Josie and I walked home for lunch which usually consisted of soup made from leftovers. Some days we ate slices of Mama's bread spread with lard and sprinkled with sugar.

Mama got milk from a farmer a little way out of town. She walked there to get it. I discovered later that she cleaned out the dairy stalls to pay for the milk, butter and eggs on our table. I realize now, we ate better than a lot of families, and Mama's garden kept us healthy.

The house consisted of a kitchen and bedroom, plus the little storage room where Josie and I slept. The toilet was outside. Evening came on, and we started watching for Daddy from the front window of their bedroom.

Mama pushed straight chairs together. It was scrunchy, but Josie and I liked sitting close to Mama, feeling warm and loved. I knew Mama was beautiful, and I would never look like her. I loved her with all my heart. While we watched some of the other daddies coming home, Mama sang tunes she was always making up. Josie sat quietly. She was a year older than I and rarely uttered a word. Mama said Josie was busy listening to the angels and would probably tell us what they had to say one of these days. Then Mama would hug both of us.

Josie and I were in the same grade at school, and one day, some of the kids called her "dummy mummy." Waiting until we were off the grounds after school, a few good punches put an end to it. My teacher, Mrs. McEnroe, sent Mama a note. Mama visited her at school. I guess they had something else to talk about. Mama never mentioned it.

The sun went down, leaving brilliant pink, blue and orange streaks in the sky. Mama stopped singing and breathed a deep sigh.

"Let's go put supper on the table."

When the Roll is Called Up Yonder

Walter sat down in his favorite rocker. He placed a banjo against the white railing of the porch. Dressed in his brown and white Sunday-go-to-meeting seersucker suit, he looked out over the manicured yard, watching the birds feed at boxes suspended from the trees. He ran his hand over a white shock of hair and checked his tie.

"Don't you look dressed fit to kill," Marcie, a care worker, said. The screen door slamming behind her. "You are some good looking fellow." She smiled and patted him on the shoulder.

"Better get your eyes checked." Walter chuckled, giving her a wink.

"Where are you off to today?"

"We're baptizing a baby at my daughter's church in Glasgow."

"You going to play your banjo?

"We'll see."

"You tell those kids of yours I said they better treat you good, or else they'll have to answer to me."

Walter shook his head. That's what Marcie told everyone at the retirement home. She was right in a lot of cases, but he didn't have any complaints. Only one of his four children, Jonie, lived within a day's visit, and she did the best she could. This baby was Jonie's fourth grandchild, Walter's sixth great-grandchild. The baby's mother, Louise, had to work to take care of her brood. Her husband had been disabled in a car accident shortly before the baby was born. Jonie, mother and grandmother, would have less time for him. The older children were growing away from him too. "But, that's the way it goes," he said to himself. "They love me in their own way."

Jonie was late, but he didn't mind. A nap would feel good. He closed his eyes and soon slept soundly. As usual, he dreamed of years gone by. A boy ran through the pasture of the family farm toward a creek. He couldn't wait to jump into the cool water. Voices he knew became louder. The memory of splashing, dunking, swimming brought a smile to his sleeping face.

Then he saw Margie walking toward him wearing her white lace wedding dress and a circlet of flowers in her hair. She smiled the slow way that always warmed his heart. He dreamed of slipping the plain gold band on her finger. She drifted away before he could kiss her.

He heard a baby crying. His heart ached. The next image was a small mound in the cemetery next to the weathered white church. Everything turned dark.

He seemed to fly about looking for something. His heart continued to ache. Suddenly he settled into a large truck filled with other young men. They wore combat clothing, helmets on their heads, rifles in their hands. He thought he recognized the faces. No one said a word. The truck rumbled over a rough road. Suddenly there was an explosion and a flash. The truck lifted off the road, scattering the men into a ditch full of water. Fire burst from the truck, and he was running as fast as he could. His heart raced. Pain shot down his arms.

Walter breathed deeply. The pain subsided. He roused for a moment but went back to sleep. He and Margie were in a hospital room. A nurse brought a small bundle and placed it in Walter's arms. "Jonie" he murmured. Another nurse came in and placed a bundle in Margie's arms. "Paul," she said. Jonie patted her little brother on the nose. Where are Tim and John, he wondered. At a tug on his trousers, he turned and saw four young faces. "Daddy," they giggled.

The light in the room dimmed. Now Walter sat beside their bed at home holding Margie's cold hand. Her eyes were closed. A young woman and three young men stood at the foot of the bed. They sobbed uncontrollably. He turned toward Margie. Now a sheet covered the face of his beloved. Pain in his head was unbearable. He took a deep breath.

Walter felt a hand on his shoulder. "Wake up. It's time to go."

"I must have dropped off," he said and reached for his banjo.

"You don't need that today. You'll be too busy."

When he turned to disagree with Jonie, he saw Margie instead, wearing a white lace dress and a circlet of flowers in her hair. She kissed him, took his hand, and they were gone.

Marcie found Walter in the rocker.

The Cat Caper

"Damn cat."

I am a sound sleeper, and it took a moment to recall that my college roommate had gone to bed cuddling a young kitten she'd found mewing under some bushes on her way back to our dorm that evening.

I turned on my lamp. "What's the matter?" I asked, not really wanting to know.

"She peed on me. My sheet is all wet." Gerry was standing beside her bed, holding the small calico away from her with both hands. It mewed loudly.

"Shut up," she commanded. When it began scratching, she put the creature on the floor. It ran under her bed.

My roommate took off her soiled pajamas, pulled the wet sheets from her bed and took the bundle into the adjoining bathroom. I got out of bed and reached for the kitten, hoping some TLC would hush the piteous sounds that were getting louder. If we were caught with a cat in our room, we'd be in all kinds of trouble. I'd tried to dissuade Gerry last evening when she told me her plan.

"There's a hard and fast rule, Gerry. No pets."

"We can't put the poor little thing outside, all alone. It's cold. Besides, it'll be okay for one night. Tomorrow we can look for her mother." She made a place in the bathroom for the cat to sleep on some of her dirty clothes. She put down a small bowl of water and the kitten lapped greedily. Gerry opened a can of Vienna sausage, and the kitten ate every one.

"Isn't she adorable?" Gerry scratched the ball of fur and crooned. "Let's call her Sweet'ums."

"What makes you think it's a she?"

Gerry ignored me and continued to caress the cat who soon fell asleep. She carried it to the bathroom and placed it on the makeshift bed. Gerry spread newspapers over the entire floor and closed the door.

"See?" She turned on her radio to music we both liked. It stopped after we were asleep, so I don't know how long it was before the caterwauling startled us awake.

"What in the?" Gerry began and then remembered. I was sure the entire floor heard the racket. Gerry opened the bathroom door and turned on the light. The kitten stopped its noise, came out and rubbed against her leg.

"My Sweet'ums is just lonesome," Gerry said. "And, she used the newspaper. What a good kitty." She gave me a look that said, "I told you so," and got into bed with the cat.

"You aren't going to sleep with it?" I asked. Apprehension gave me goosebumps.

"Of course. She's a baby and misses her mommy."

"What if she has to pee?"

"When she moves, I'll wake up and take her to the bathroom."

And that was that until Gerry's snarling awakened me. She gasped as the kitten streaked from under the bed.

"Oh, shit."

That's what it was. A trail of feces flecked with bits of Vienna sausage swept across the floor to the bathroom. The smell was out of proportion to the amount of excrement. Gerry ran and slammed the door. I was certain the floor monitor would be down any minute. But no one came. It was just us and that damn cat.

"What are you going to do?" I asked trying to emphasize "you."

"We have to put it outside." There was no hesitation in her voice. The "we" was like a mild electric jolt, and my sense of self-preservation surfaced.

"How are you going to do that? We're on the fourth floor. The doors are locked. Open one, and the fire alarm goes off. If we get caught with this cat ..." I didn't finish. My stomach churned. I saw my diploma burning to a crisp and my sacrificing parents dying of shame.

Gerry ignored me and wrapped the kitten in a towel to avoid the tiny claws as well as to mute the meowing. She slipped on a bathrobe and told me to do the same. Opening the door to our room, she looked to see if anyone was about.

"Come on," she hissed and pulled me out into the hall. We crept down the stairs, forgoing the elevator that would have awakened the housemother. Below the entry level of the building was a daylight basement that housed the dining hall, kitchen and various equipment and maintenance rooms. When we reached the lower level, I said, "What are you going to do?"

"Find a window," she snapped. The cat was quiet, and I wondered if it was still alive.

The door to the dining hall and kitchen was locked. We began trying doors to various rooms along a narrow hall. Locked, locked, locked, open. The janitor had forgotten to lock his door. Dim lights in the hallway enabled us to see a window at the end of a narrow aisle between cleaning supplies and equipment.

"Oh, God," Gerry whispered. "Please."

I found the latch and pushed. Surprisingly, there was no screen for us to vandalize.

"Quick," I said. "I think I hear the security patrol car coming." I didn't but was afraid Gerry might change her mind. I sighed with relief when she dropped the swaddled kitten to the ground and slammed the window shut. I turned the latch.

The next day we searched the grounds, but there was no kitten. Just the towel, dirty and reeking.

Some months later, as I walked to the dorm, I passed the door to the kitchen. A woman was putting food scraps into a shallow bowl while a calico cat sat nearby.

The Red Hat

"That's it!" she exclaimed.

Hurrying across the department store aisle to where the hats were displayed, she stood and looked at the skimmer that had caught her eye.

"Buy me," it seemed to say.

"I will, I will," she whispered.

"I want to try on that one," she said to the approaching saleslady, pointing.

The woman carefully removed the hat from its display stand and took it over to a small table with a triptych mirror. She gave the teenager a hand mirror so the girl could see how it looked from all angles.

The bright red, woven straw was fashioned into a flat, shallow crown and a wide, flat brim. A pale beige taffeta ribbon with white polka dots wrapped around the crown, and the flat bow was attached to the side of the crown with two streamers lying across the brim.

"You can wear the bow to the side or to the back," the saleslady advised.

She placed the hat squarely on her head. She tipped it to the back; a little to the left, a little to the right. She liked the bow to the side.

"This style is very chic," said the saleslady.

"I am lovely," the hat whispered.

"I'll take it."

She wore it out of the store, trying to glimpse her reflection in the shop windows. Each time she saw the hat she smiled with satisfaction and happiness.

She felt free as a bird. This was the first time her mother had allowed her to shop alone and buy what she wanted. Her stomach did a slight tilt when she remembered how much the hat cost. She hadn't thought to ask the price because she had known the hat was destined to be hers. The saleslady assured her it was a classic style. "Though the red makes a strong statement, the beige ribbon gives it an elegance that will go with everything."

As she made her way to the cafeteria where her mother was waiting, she heard a low, soft whistle behind her. She didn't look around because that would have been unladylike, but her heart gave a thump, and her face felt tingly. Soon a tall, well dressed, very handsome man came past, looked back at her, tipped his hat and smiled broadly.

Oh, my goodness! she thought. Is it the hat? No one had ever whistled at her or looked at her in such a romantically suggestive way. He reminded her of Clark Gable.

When she strode through the cafeteria door, her mother looked up and saw a short, slightly overweight sixteen-year-old, wearing a floral green and yellow dress, white flat slippers and white anklets, all topped off with a large red straw hat like one Joan Crawford had worn in a recent movie. Mother took a deep breath and smiled warmly.

"I see you've done your shopping, Doreen. What a lovely hat."

"I am lovely," whispered the hat.

Who Was That Man?

Amanda's husband, Grady, dropped dead on the 15th hole. Their daughter, Clarrie, helped sort his clothing and deliver it to the thrift shop. Dan took his dad's golf equipment to the high school. Amanda didn't mention the file cabinet in her husband's home office. She wasn't up to anymore going through his things and giving them away. Grady called the home files his "second copy," referring to business files in his downtown insurance office.

I still don't see why he was so secretive about them, Amanda thought. He'd kept the cabinet locked, and she never saw the key. It wasn't on his key chain, in his desk or other places where he'd stashed things. Today she'd decided to give his room a good cleaning and forget about the file cabinet. First, she dusted the framed certificates attesting to his success as an insurance salesman. When she turned the first one over, there was a small sealed envelope attached to the back. What in the world! She looked inside the envelope and found what looked like a file cabinet key. She tried it, but it didn't fit. She removed another certificate. It, too, had an envelope with a key that didn't fit. She quickly discovered that each certificate had an envelope and key. They all looked like file cabinet keys.

I'll be darned. She smiled, remembering. When he worked in his home office, Grady locked the door, so that one had to knock. He said he focused so completely on his work, it would ruin his pace if someone came barging in. Sometimes he didn't answer. She understood when the children were young and rambunctious. She'd become used to it and rarely knocked on the door, attributing his one idiosyncrasy to having been an only child.

Amanda spread the keys on the desk and saw they were all different. Grady Lewis. What were you thinking? Finally, she found the key that fit. The top drawer was filled with folders of personal memorabilia from his school days, including high school and college yearbooks. She had no idea he cared about such things.

Amanda pulled out the second and third drawers which were jammed with bulging manila folders. One was labeled: Plot for "The Magnificent Stranger." The others were similarly labeled: "Lost in Lust," "A Woman's Heart," and various bodice ripper titles. She counted thirty-five folders. The fourth drawer contained correspondence and copies of contracts. They were made out to Maureen Van Dahlen.

Amanda plopped on the floor and began breathing deeply. She knew it would take awhile to get used to the idea that her husband was also her favorite author.

U-Turn

Cassie slowed when she saw the unfamiliar cross street sign, Bane Road. She checked the rearview mirror. Seeing no traffic from either direction, she made a U-turn and headed back to Pike Road where she should have taken a right. I've never done that before, she thought. She drove to work this way every day. This morning her mind was on the meeting scheduled with the Wilmots, whose vacation home she was trying to sell. That will be a nice commission, she thought. Maybe we can get away for a real vacation. A Caribbean cruise might help us put things the way they should be.

Cassie was beginning to wonder how far she'd driven past Pike Road. She sped up. "I don't remember those older houses," she said. "They're farther from the street on larger lots. Where's the sidewalk? There's a rural mailbox. Where's Pike Road?"

The street curved sharply and became a narrow, graveled road. Tall trees formed a canopy through which the morning sun sent long streaks of pale light. "It's like a cathedral," she whispered. Her skin tingled. Something skittered across the road. Cassie hit the brakes. The car slid in the loose gravel, then stopped with a thump as the right rear wheel dropped. She accelerated. The car didn't move. Cassie got out and saw the tire wedged in a ditch overgrown with weeds. She reached for her cell phone and punched the key for emergency road help.

"Where are you located?" asked the dispatcher.

"I'm not sure." Cassie tried to explain how she'd driven to this unfamiliar place.

"Ma'am, I have to have an address or directions with landmarks."

Cassie hit the button and sat for a moment. "I don't know where I am." She turned the car key. No response. "I'd better start walking."

When Cassie headed back, the sunlight was gone, and a soft drizzle began to fall. Her lightweight cloth jacket absorbed the moisture. She shivered from anxiety as well as the dampness. "I think there was a house before the road turned and became gravel," she murmured.

The way back was longer than she remembered. "This gravel is chewing up my shoes." Cassie's right ankle turned and a sharp pain shot through her leg. Everything went black before she hit the ground.

"Cassie, what are you doing on the floor?" Dylan's voice was unsympathetic.

After a week, Cassie was able to drive to work in spite of the sprained ankle. Dylan had driven her grudgingly, claiming that he needed all the time he could get to find a job. He'd been laid off recently from a computer company. Cassie had no idea of the circumstances. He called his coworkers "a bunch of jerks." It was his third firing in four years.

As Cassie drove along the familiar route, she thought about the Gundersons who were considering purchasing the Wilmots' vacation home. They seemed to really want the house but were delaying. "I wonder what the problem is? Oh, darn. I've passed Pike Road," she said as she saw the Bane Road sign. Cassie checked the rearview mirror. Seeing no traffic from either direction, she made a U-turn. As she retraced her way, she recalled the morning she'd fallen out of bed after the dream in which she became lost. She hadn't thought about it since, and the details had faded.

Cassie's heart began to beat faster when she couldn't find Pike Road. The dream emerged more clearly when she noticed the older houses looked familiar. No sidewalks. Rural mailboxes. As in her dream, the suburban street turned sharply and became a narrow, graveled country road. Tall trees formed a canopy, reminding her of the long slanting rays that made her think of a cathedral. Cassie stopped the car carefully. "If this is a dream, I don't have to do anything." The car motor idled. "But maybe this isn't a dream." Her heart skipped a beat. "I'd better not just sit here."

Cassie was afraid to turn around on the narrow road and risk slipping into the ditch on either side. She drove slowly. "This road must go somewhere." It curved sharply in an S. Suddenly a long, narrow wooden bridge stretched before her. She saw no stream, just the impenetrable forest, now softened by a drizzle. She stopped the car, took a deep breath and slowly drove onto the bridge. After several minutes, she realized that the end of the bridge didn't seem to be getting any closer. "I don't like this," she said. "I'll just back my way out." When she put the gear in reverse, the car jerked sideways, creasing the left front fender against the side railing of the bridge. The motor stalled. The weathered wood creaked loudly. Cassie clutched the steering wheel. "Don't panic," she told herself. She turned the key. No response.

The driver's door was wedged against the railing and wouldn't open all the way. She managed to squeeze through, pulled up the hood of her coat and began to walk. When she neared the gravel road, a plank gave way. Her left foot went through a hole. The leather boot protected her lower leg, but she landed on her knee, Pain raced through her hip and torso. She collapsed onto the bridge, hitting her head on the timber railing. Just as unconsciousness began to overtake her, she heard heavy footsteps on the bridge. A large hand brushed the strands of hair from her forehead. The skin felt coarse, but the touch was gentle, warm and smelled of cedar. She was unable to open her eyes.

A deep, gentle voice was the last thing she heard. "Why must you always turn back?"

Cassie awoke in the hospital. She lay with her eyes closed, slowly remembering the events that led up to her fall on the bridge. She felt the gentle touch on her cheek. Before she had time to sort it out, the door flew open, and a scowling Dylan strode in.

Her husband plopped on the foot of the bed, sending arrows of pain through her knee. "I think you're becoming accident prone, you know that? The car's a mess."

Cassie turned away. He doesn't care if I'm okay, just the car.

"I talked to the insurance company," he said. "Our rates will go up. How did you manage to hit the side of Moss Evans Bridge? You were the only one on it."

"What do you mean?" She turned toward him, holding back tears.

"According to witnesses, you stopped, turned your wheel and smashed into the railing. You got out and fell down. You must have hit your head. You were out like a light. Doctor says nothing shows on the x-ray, but he thinks you have a slight concussion. Your knee isn't broken. The pulled muscles are what hurt. You can go home tomorrow. He wants to see you in two weeks. Says you can go back to work when you feel like it. I get to be your chauffeur, again." He didn't try to hide the displeasure in his voice or face. Cassie closed her eyes and pretended to doze. Dylan left.

Two weeks later, Cassie sat at the kitchen table and poured herself a second cup of coffee. She thought back over the last six months. Sometimes she knew what ticked him off, other times there wasn't a clue. Dylan had become demanding, insensitive, distant. When his outbursts became daily, she suggested counseling. He refused. Since the accident, silence and short answers told her how he felt about having to do things around the apartment and take her back and forth to work every day. Sometimes he was late. No apology. She no longer asked if he'd been on a job interview. She usually smelled beer on his breath.

Cassie hobbled into the bathroom on crutches and saw a business card lying on the floor. Using a grabber, she retrieved the small item. Below the name of Dylan's favorite sports bar, it read: "Maxine Miller, Manager" A residential address, telephone number, and 10 AM, underlined, was written on the reverse side. Cassie felt sick to her stomach. I thought he was stressed about not finding a job. My being the primary moneymaker has always bothered him. Now, this. She threw the card on the floor, finished dressing and went out to her car. Driving with one good leg was difficult, but doable.

Cassie drove toward her doctor's appointment that was on the way to her office. She saw the sign for Pike Road and drove past. When she approached Bane Road, she slowed, checked the rearview mirror. Seeing no traffic from either direction, Cassie made a U-turn.

Yield Not to Temptation

"Yield not to temptation, for yielding is sin," the congregation sang. Ben listened to the words of the old hymn that he had known for seventy plus years. Though it wasn't sung often these days, whenever Ben heard it, he was ten years old again and wanted a bicycle more than anything in the world. When his tenth birthday came and there was no bicycle, he couldn't hide his disappointment.

"Son, times are hard for us right now," his father said. "Maybe next year,"

One Saturday afternoon, Ben was walking home and thinking about the bicycle he wanted. It was red with silvery aluminum fenders and a guard over the chain to keep your pants from getting caught. A warning bell was attached to the handlebar. He imagined himself riding up and down the streets and the admiring looks of his friends.

When he passed the Wilsons' large white house, he glanced up the sloping driveway that led to the garage. The doors were closed, but Ben knew about the creamy tan Airflow Studebaker sitting in there. Most every man in town wanted a car like that, including Ben's father who wouldn't admit it. The front door of the house was closed. Drapes covered the bay window

Ben was about to go past when he glimpsed something shiny lying in the grass just off the driveway. He walked up the slight incline. There it was. A new red bicycle with aluminum fenders, a chain guard and a bell on the handlebar lay as though someone had carelessly thrown it down.

"I wonder what that bell sounds like," he whispered. He gave it a squeeze. A loud demanding ring startled him. Ben expected Henry Wilson to come running out and get him. Henry, at eleven, was tall for his age and mean beyond his years. Ben retreated to the sidewalk, but no one appeared.

"Looks like no one's home. I'll just take another gander. Don't hurt to look," Ben said to himself.

Looking became spinning the upturned wheel, another ring of the bell and then pulling the bicycle upright onto the driveway. It began to roll down the incline with Ben hanging on until they were both in the street. He managed to stop the roll and tried to direct the bike back into the drive, but it seemed to have a mind of its own. The bicycle wanted to roll along the curb following the descent of the street. To keep it from getting away, Ben managed to jump onto the seat. He found the pedals and soon had everything under control.

He thought how lucky he was that there were no cars on the street, and the few people out in their yards didn't seem to notice. A boy on a bicycle wasn't unusual.

Suddenly he realized he'd taken Henry's bike out of his yard and was riding away. "Thou shalt not steal!" he remembered. The shock was such that he lost control of the bike, and it crashed into the curb. Ben fell beneath it. At first, he thought he was dead because the pain was everywhere. Then he saw the bent front wheel and wished he were.

Ben soon realized that the pain was from scrapes to his legs and arms as well as a good bump on the head, but nothing seemed to be broken. Again, he had escaped notice and tried to think of what to do. He knew he had to take the bike back but hoped no one was home yet.

How can I ever tell Henry? Or my dad? They'll get me good.

Ben picked up the wreck and managed to roll it back to the Wilsons' driveway. It seemed that no one was home, but when he placed the bicycle where he'd found it, the front door of the house opened.

"Hi, Benji." It was Ellen, Henry's ten-year-old sister. Skinny, freckled and red curly hair. He hated being called Benji.

She came out to the drive and looked at the bicycle.

"I saw you ride off. What happened?" She grinned as though this was the best thing she'd seen in a long time. Ben explained as clearly and honestly as he could.

"I didn't intend to keep it. Just wanted to see how good it rode. I'm real sorry about the wheel. Is Henry here? I guess I'd better tell him." He grimaced and shivered at the thought.

"He and my folks are over to Wilburville," Ellen told him. "Grandma's babysitting me, but she's napping." The little girl giggled. "I don't know when they'll be back." She continued looking at the bike and then said. "Tell you what, Benji. You don't have to wait for them. You look pretty scraped up and all. I'll explain everything. Henry can talk to you later. Okay?" She smiled at him and patted him on the shoulder.

Ben was glad he didn't have to face Henry right away, so he thanked Ellen and went home. He got into the house without his mother seeing the scrapes. He washed them and put on a long-sleeved shirt. He stayed in his room until dinner. His head throbbed, but he got through the evening and to bed with no questions.

The next morning in church, they sang, "Yield Not to Temptation." Ben scrunched down in the pew.

The following Monday at school, Ben was surprised that Henry didn't confront him, though there were several opportunities. Finally, he spoke to Ellen.

"Henry hasn't said anything to me."

"Why should he?"

"Well, you know. About his bicycle.? Saturday?"

"Yes, that was too bad, but Papa said it was Henry's fault for leaving his bike out like that where just anyone could get it. He said Henry was lucky that whoever it was brought it back even after ruining the wheel."

Ben stared at the grinning girl in disbelief.

"By the way, Benji, Mama says you can come to my Valentine's Day party next Friday. Bye now."

Ben roused from his reverie as the hymn ended, "Look ever to Jesus, He'll carry you through." The minister gave the benediction. A hand softly touched Ben on the shoulder.

"Come along, Benji. We have to get home before the children arrive for dinner."

"Right, Ellen, right." Ben smiled up at a mature, very pretty, red-haired woman.

Two Hearts

"Come on, old woman. We got to get home 'fore dark." Walter, tall, gaunt, stepped from the front door of the shop and headed for his pickup truck parked across the street. He wore blue overalls and a green and white checked shirt, both clean and faded from many washings. A broad-brimmed straw hat, sweat-stained on the band, covered a shock of white hair.

The small, slender woman to whom he'd spoken gathered her packages from the counter and placed them in a woven basket. She tucked a tendril of brown hair that had escaped the bun on the nape of her neck.

"Thank you, Jenny. Good to see you, Ora Mae." She smiled and hurried to catch up with her husband.

"That old codger," said the owner of Jenny's Fabric and Notions.

"I've never seen that man smile," said Ora Mae Miller. "I've always wondered what kind of life she has out there with him on that farm. After William and James went into the Navy, you'd have thought he'd cut back some. My Marvin says he hires a few seasonal workers, but he and Susan do the rest."

"She's still a pretty thing. Poor Susan." Jenny and Ora Mae shook their heads.

Walter turned the truck onto the dirt lane that led to their home. On either side were rows of tall cornstalks almost ready for harvesting. Three large dogs of varied breed and color greeted them and ran beside the truck. Surrounded by a low white picket fence containing a profusion of bright flowers and two oak trees was their white frame house.

Walter drove around to the back and unloaded boxes and paper bags. Susan took her basket from the front seat and went through the kitchen into the bedroom. She paused at a freestanding quilters frame holding royal blue satin squares joined with narrow red strips. The white middle square held two gold stars. She brushed away the tears that always came. "I'll have you finished soon." She put the basket underneath the table and hurried from the room.

In the kitchen, Susan put away grocery items in the pantry and refrigerator. At that end of the large room were polished maple cabinets, up-to-date appliances and a large butcher block in the center. A window behind the sink looked out at the barn and a chicken pen with several coops. At the other end of the room, a large bay window looked out to cultivated fields that rolled away into a dense woodland. Two recliner loungers afforded a continuing, changing view. They ate at a table in the center of the room. Walter had crafted the kitchen cabinets as well as shelves that reached the ceiling, filled with books, National Geographic, family pictures and mementos.

When Walter came in after seeing to the stock, Susan was putting dinner on the table. They folded their hands and bowed their heads in a moment of silence. The knives and forks clinked occasionally, but quietness wrapped them in a cocoon of intimacy and familiarity with no need to speak. When they finished, Susan reached for Walter's empty plate. He brushed her wrist with his fingers. She touched his forehead with her lips.

A bit later, the dishwasher hummed as the two of them sat comfortably looking out the window. The sun had already gone down over the distant hills, leaving swishes of purple, yellow and orange across the sky. The fields changed into varied shades of green.

"You know this day, don't you?" Walter said.

"Yes. I've remembered them. Like we do every day."

"Our boys are at rest. Too soon."

"I miss them so." Susan brushed a tear from her cheek.

"We always will." Walter reached for her hand.

They read for a while, then turned out the lights. In the bedroom, they stood at the table and looked at the quilt.

"It's almost finished," Susan said. Walter pulled her gently toward him and held her for a long moment. Susan settled her head on his chest.

Later when Walter entered their bedroom, Susan was sitting on the side of their bed wearing a granny gown. Her feet didn't touch the floor. He knelt in front of his wife and began to massage her feet, ankles and lower legs with a soothing cream. He felt the tightness give in and knew the pain would go away, for a while.

Walter got into bed and switched off the lamp. He pulled up his pajama top and lay on his stomach. Susan squeezed some of the cream onto the muscles in her husband's back. She used pressure in a smooth up and down stroke across his shoulders and torso. She felt him relax and knew to stop.

Susan turned onto her right side away from him. Walter turned toward her, holding his wife as he had all the many years.

"Goodnight, old woman."

"Goodnight, old man."

Irene Ebel Ertell

Published Writing

Books

Roscoe Ann, 2015

Ebel Hornshu Sturm, A Family Story, 2015

Potpourri, 2018

Short Stories

Guardian Spirit, 2013

Upper Left Edge

Around the Corner, 2017

Reflections, a Collection of Writing and Poetry by Oregon's Elders

Two Hearts, 2018

Reflections, a Collection of Writing and Poetry by Oregon's Elders, Judges' Choice

Flash the Northern Flicker, 2018

Upper Left Edge

River of Escape, 2018

Upper Left Edge